Message for Linda

The story and characters
are totally fictional and
any similarity to real
life is purely coincidental

author   t. a. wood

cover illustrated by katie orchard

MESSAGE

For

LINDA

by t. a. wood

INTRODUCTION

An internet article regarding her father's camera lost about forty years ago in Switzerland arouses Linda's interest leading to devasting consequences to herself and her family. Against her father's advice she is tempted to reply to the author who is offering it's return together with the film.
Consequently she is taken hostage and the search for her takes many different routes. At one stage even sending her parents from their home on the west coast of Scotland to the place where it was lost in the hope of finding her.

.

printed in larger text for easier reading

MESSAGE for LINDA

Chapter One

The repeated chimes of Westminster emanating from the door bell caused Joseph to lift himself from the comfort of his chair in the lounge and hurry into his darkened hallway. He paused momentarily for a few seconds and only opening the front door when he recognised his daughter's voice shouting excitedly from the other side.

"Linda, what the hell are you doing here at this time of the night, are you on your own ?"

"No, Tom's with me, he's just getting Blanche out of car".

Linda, once an uncontrollable tearaway, now a petite attractive forty six year old woman, albeit still carrying a chip on her shoulder, adopted by Joseph and his wife when she was fourteen years old after they had been her foster parents for the previous two tumultuous years, stood holding the door open while their enormous white King German Shepherd dog dragged her husband Thomas into the house to be followed by her father back into the lounge where he promptly sat back into his chair.

Bubbling with excitement Linda dashed Into her father's study.

"What are you looking for in there ?"

Joseph called out.

"I'm looking for your laptop".

"You won't find it in there, it's on the coffee table in the conservatory. What do you want it for ?"

Linda collected the machine and clicked onto the Facebook page and scrolled down for a good five minutes anxiously willing the screen to provide the article she was searching for.

"Who do you reckon that fella' is then Joe ?" Linda screeched gleefully

"Well it looks like a young me. Damn me it is me with some of my army mates. But what on earth is this picture doing on here ?" Joseph asked impatiently.

"I knew it was, I told you so didn't I ?" He wouldn't have it". Linda snapped, turning and giving her husband Thomas a satisfactory smirk.

"When it came up on the internet I found out an old photo album, I knew I had a picture of you in your army uniform. You gave me the album and lots of photos as a present on the day you and Jane adopted me". Linda gushed with ever more excitement.

"This photograph of me on the internet must have been taken when I was stationed in Germany. The bloke with the three stripes on his arms leaning on my shoulder is a chap named Knowles, he was my best army mate all the while I was in Germany. Harry Knowles......Knowles'y from Bradford. He got promoted to Staff Sergeant just after I arrived on the base. Good God some of these photos are nearly fifty years old. I remember taking these pictures, I'd just had a new camera, my parents sent it to me at the camp for my twenty first birthday in nineteen seventy".

"Nearly all these pictures are photos I took on the military base, the others all seem to be taken on a skiing holiday in Switzerland. I think I look fantastic in that shot, a real professional in all that gear. Yes I was a good skier before you ask". Joseph said slightly exaggerating his ability on the slopes and noting the look of utter disbelief on Linda's face. "I lost the roll of film so how the hell has it come up on here ?" He added looking towards his daughter for the answer.

"There's still a few more photos you haven't seen". Linda announced as she repeatedly clicked on to the arrow on the right hand side of the picture in view.

Joseph pulled the computer to his side of the table and proceeded to view the pictures again, still spluttering his words in amazement at seeing photos he never expected to see.

Linda quickly retrieved the computer from her father's grip and turned it back in her direction. "There's only the one comment. It says someone recently found a very expensive camera and hopefully in order to trace whoever has lost it, they had the film developed and they would be pleased if the owner would make contact, or anyone who can recognise any of the people in the photographs. Oh….." Linda paused. "This is a very old post, look at the original date. August two thousand and eight. Facebook must have regenerated it". Linda moaned in dismay.

"Does it happen to say where they found it ?" Joseph asked, deeply suspicious regarding any answer.

"I'll read the rest of the comment if you'll stop tugging at the laptop. Yes, Some hill walkers came across it buried in the undergrowth near the village of Grindelwald in Switzerland. So how did it get there then Joe ?" Linda asked and swiftly carried on talking without giving her father the chance to answer.

Linda had a broad cheeky grin on her face as she viewed the pictures again making the same remark each time a photo featuring a particular girl appeared on the screen. "Wow ! her again…….who is this rather gorgeous looking young female Joe ?" Linda quipped with a mischievous look of curiosity while smiling suspiciously at her father waiting for his response, still reluctant to refer to him as dad.

Joseph chose to ignore his daughter's craftily loaded insinuations, but peered over the shoulders of her and his son–in–law viewing the pictures for a third time. He stared at the girl in the final picture as it remained on the screen and decided the only way to satisfy Linda's curiosity was to tell all, as he found himself captivated by the girl in the photograph uncannily appearing to be staring back at him.

"Alright.......you're not going to let it rest until I've told you, but for goodness sake don't you dare say anything to your mum when she gets back home. Or suggest I show her the photos". Joseph insisted.

Linda's husband Thomas returned to his preferred position of the isolated upright dining chair in the far corner of the lounge, carefully stepping over Blanche as she slept peacefully where he'd left her.

Thomas, a smooth handsome forty eight year old man with sleek dark hair, standing six feet two inches high with the build of a champion weight lifter and at the moment sporting a silly sinister looking pencil thin line of dark bristle above his top lip which had been irritating Joseph ever since they arrived until eventually Joseph couldn't resist the temptation to ask his daughter if Clark Gable would like a cup of coffee. Only to receive the reply 'Who's Clark Gable". "I'll make some coffee anyway". He quipped and wandered off into the kitchen.

"Oh yes, and why don't you want Jane to see the pictures, what had you been up to". Linda asked winking cheekily the minute her father returned with a tray of drinks.

"Nothing.......nothing at all, but I do have my reasons and your mother would be very upset to find out that I hadn't told her much about the girl and she might not be too happy if she sees her in most of the pictures. My life probably wouldn't be worth living for a couple of weeks".

"Why's that then, why would she be upset. Was this thing with Elena before or after you met Jane ?" Linda quizzed.

Joseph now a gentleman of sixty nine years, still a good looking fellow. A slight bald patch beginning to surface at the back of his head, but cleverly hidden by his otherwise mass of blonde to greying hair. Always freshly shaven, smart and always neatly dressed as ever, even when working in his garden or just loafing around the house. A modest man with several distinctive titles and letters after his name which he chooses to keep private. Refusing to be drawn into his daughter's web and craftily dodging her searching questions, and to deflect her next stage in the inquisition he began to recall as to how he came to lose the camera.

"As I said before, the camera was a

present from my parents for my twenty first birthday, they sent it out to me when I was stationed in Germany. I can't believe how it managed to survive for forty years, let alone how the film was still printable".

"No, it didn't survive forty years in the undergrowth, it was found in two thousand and eight, so it was only thirty years". Linda interrupted with her wisdom.

"Well alright.....thirty years then, still a long time exposed to the rain, snow and ice in that country. But it must have done, well the film did, otherwise we wouldn't have it on here". Joseph uttered as he tapped the closed lid of the silver computer. "I was annoyed at losing the damn thing, being my twenty first present. And I know it cost my parents more than hundred quid to get it for me. That was a good lot of money in those days. It was a Zeiss Ikon, made by a German company of all things. Even though it was in a very sturdy leather case I still don't believe any camera would be any good after thirty years. Seems strange that the film survived somehow, well it did, we've just seen the photos".

Joseph paused to think of a more plausible tale than what actually happened, but relented as his mind fell blank and proceeded with the true version. "We were on a two seater chairlift on the first section of a trip up to the top of some mountain when a very strong gust of wind caught my friend's hat and I stupidly let go my camera and made a grab for it and the camera fell from my lap. I watched it bounce off the safety bar and vanish into the woods below".

"Who was the other half of the 'we' I bet it was one of the girls ?" Linda chirped.

"Yes it was one of the girls, she was Austrian, named Elena. Okay....now are you satisfied ?" Joseph snapped half serious and half in jest.

"Elena eh ! And what happened to Elena's hat then ?" Thomas, the Clark Gable lookalike asked jokingly as he stood from his chair and came and sat next to his wife on the settee to be more engaged in the conversation, disturbing Blanche from her comfortable position. The extra sized dog followed Thomas and instinctively obeyed his instruction to 'sit'.

"Oh, she managed to hang on to it". Joseph replied with a slight tone of guilt.

"So while the gorgeous Elena was saving her knitted wooly bobble hat you lost a hundred quid worth German camera. Typical ! gallant Joe strikes again". Linda laughed. "What was wrong with having the strap around your neck ? I assume it had one". She added scornfully.

"I had no intention of walking about looking like a tourist with it dangling across my chest". Joseph replied indignantly.

"You silly bugger". Linda grunted in disgust.

"Anyway that's all in the past, water under the bridge now. Do you want me to carry on ?" Joseph retorted sarcastically. "Oh, by the way, if you're wondering, your mum obviously knows I lost the camera but I told her that I was on the chairlift with my mate Harry Knowles. And I never told your grandparents that I'd even lost it. You won't be able to tell your granddad, but next time you see your grandma don't mention anything. I doubt if she'd remember anyway".

Joseph poured himself a glass of white wine and took a sip before continuing. "We were on a skiing holiday, I was due to be sent back home a few weeks later to be discharged from the army and transferred to a top secret military establishment up here in Scotland, but me and a couple of my mates, Knowles'y was one, we had some leave still owed to us, so we booked this holiday in a hotel in a mountain village near Grindelwald in Switzerland. I couldn't see any point dashing back home just for a few days leave and having to pay my own way when Her Majesty was sending me back to the UK a month later". Joseph felt his mouth beginning to dry and after a couple of throaty coughs he broke off his story to sip from his wine glass before continuing. By now he realised that he had begun to relish in reliving his younger and carefree days.

"We got friendly with a group of girls staying in our hotel and I got lumbered with this girl Elena. For the first couple of days we all went skiing and knocked around together, then we seemed to drift off as couples".

"Oh, yer, How unfortunate for you to get lumbered....I do like that word lumbered ....and ?" Linda chuntered sarcastically with a wry smile.

Joseph smiled back at his daughter and ignored her cheeky comment.

"You can see that most of the photos were taken on the base, the first few are almost fifty years ago. The others are a bit boring, they're the skiing holiday".

"Well you don't look that bored sitting holding hands with the delicious Elena, she seems to be in every picture. I bet she put a stop to you admiring the mountain scenery". Linda intervened with a brazen laugh.

"Cheeky sod....Yes, she was rather a lovely looking girl, just a pity regarding her motives". Joseph added and quickly tried to disguise his unintentional comment with a forced laugh, but his daughter latched on to it and interrupted again.

"Motives ! what about her motives ? She wasn't ?"

"No..no..no, for God's sake. Nothing

of the sort".

"Did you keep in touch?" Linda asked in her thirst for more details.

"No we didn't keep in touch, there was never any intention of it becoming a romance. She wouldn't have given her address if I asked her for it, but I already knew from one of the other girls that she wasn't with their group and that she actually lived at the hotel. It was her parents, the Maiers, who owned the place"

"Now you're beginning to intrigue me. She sounds very mysterious, I bet she was a spy, she looks like a spy, she's certainly someone you couldn't resist". Linda joked totally unaware of how close to the truth her words were. "And did you ever try to contact her again?" She repeated still determined to extract the very last drop of information.

"I did try, but not while I was still in Germany. But when I was back home in England I rang the hotel from camp where I was waiting for my release. Once I was out of the army me and your mum had a short holiday to get married and then we upped sticks and left the Midlands for a new life in this house on the Scottish coast, and I started to work in my new job with the Ministry of Defense, just a forty minute drive away. Your mum retired from the civil service and started a part time job down on the sea front in a café". Joseph uttered and paused in anticipation of another of his daughter's interruptions.

"And......back to my question". Linda demanded.

"One of these days I'll tell you the truth about her, and her parents. I did try just the once to contact her from the transit camp while waiting to be demobbed but I wasn't allowed to speak to her. Her father answered the phone and asked me not to try to contact his daughter as she had already started seeing someone. I said that didn't bother me at all and I told him that me and Elena were just friends and that I was getting married in a couple of weeks time anyway. He said Elena and her new friend would probably be leaving Switzerland. Then he sneakily asked if I knew where my next posting would be. Somehow he knew I was in the forces and that I was being released. I was surprised that Elena had a boyfriend, she never said, not that I was romantically interested in her by any means" Joseph insisted before dealing with another "Oh....yer". From his daughter..

"I wonder why he didn't want you to contact Elena".

"I assume he wanted her to keep safe and away from his activities". Joseph replied.

"What activities ? Now you are making me suspicious. Was the Maiers' spies ?".Linda said and then commented sarcastically. "Is all this tale true Joe ?....You've got a damn good memory if it is".

"There's bugger all wrong with my memory young lady". Joseph snapped and then followed it with a broad grin.

"And did she ever contact you ? Do you think she ever married this boyfriend ?"

"How should I know, I just said I never gave him any information. I know why he wanted my details and I know he already knew all about me and my work". Joseph replied knowing he needed to be more cautious in what he was saying, leaving Linda and her husband with wide open mouths desperate for more information.

"I really do think you're making a lot of this up now". Linda quipped. "Come on, you must tell, you can't just leave it at that. Was Elena's parents spies ?"

"Stop now Linda ! It's probably all a matter of fact by now but just in case, I can't say any more, one day I'll tell you. I might have already said far to much for my own good. So don't breath a word of anything I've said to anyone. Okay !"

"Alright but you must have fancied the lovely Elena". Linda continued in a jovial vane.

"No....well perhaps just a little bit. I'd already met your mum long before then, and she could outshine any girl".

"That must have took you by surprise when her dad said that she already had a fella'. At first I thought you were cheating on Jane".

"Linda, call me Joe by all means, but your mum would love you to call her mum". Joseph pleaded and carried on saying. "It wasn't anything like what's in your mind, one day you'll finally realise". Linda let out a loud screech. "When!" And then added. "Just joking".

"It's this lousy official secrets act again I suppose". She tutted and suggested. "Shall I message the author and find out if he's still around and what he wants to do?"

"No...No you won't....leave it". Joseph ordered vehemently, causing Linda to look astonished and immediately question his objection.

"Don't ask any more questions....just leave it alone, forget it! Do as I say!" Joseph repeated his demand with even more aggression. Linda shook her head bewildered and looked across the room at her husband Thomas, hoping for some support. "I'd get more encouragement from the dog than him". She cursed as Thomas remained silent.

Eventually Thomas rose to his feet and gave Blanche a slight tug on her lead.

"Do as your dad says, anyway come on it's getting late and this dog still needs

18

a walk". Thomas urged as he collected his wife's coat and tossed it onto the back of her chair.

"Bossy sod". Linda griped. "To look at him you wouldn't know he was once on the stage in the West End. He did six months in The Mousetrap until he decided to take the cheese. That's another career we'd sooner not talk about" She added, scornfully laughing at her husband and then trying another attempt to persuade her father to reveal more.

"Alright then Joe, but I really don't understand why you won't at least let me try and get your camera back. I'm sure whoever originally , or it could be more recent by someone, would be happy to see it returned to it's owner".

"My God Linda, you do go on". Joseph interrupted.

Linda wished her father goodnight with a frustrated sigh and left him standing in the open doorway watching as their car reversed from his driveway and until their rear lights disappeared from view.

****

Chapter Two

"It's still there on Facebook". Linda announced to Thomas over breakfast.

"Oh, for goodness sake don't start all over again". Thomas snapped still exhausted from the night before.

"I wonder why Joe doesn't want me to do anything, seems odd to me, not to want his camera back. If only for the sake of curiosity. I can understand why he doesn't want Jane to see some of those pictures. My what a beauty, that Elena girl".

"Well he sounded pretty emphatic about it to me, so forget it and let me finish my breakfast in peace".

"Jane gets home tomorrow, I'll pop over to see her. See if she can get him to change his mind". Linda uttered.

"That's the last thing he'll want you to do. He's already told you not to mention anything to your mum. Thomas retorted angrily, while rapidly losing patience with his wife.

"We'll see, I'll give him a ring a bit later on this morning to see what sort of mood he's in". Lind suggested apprehensively.

"I don't think that's such a good idea either, just be careful what you say. You know he's obviously got a good reason for what he said. It's bound to have something to do with his work", Thomas responded.

"Work! It's about time he bloody well retired....Robotic industry...working all hours and coming seventy. What's he thinking about. Jane deserves his time now before it's too late. I can't remember the last time they had a holiday together. Or even when they went out for an evening". Linda screeched annoyingly, causing the dog to sharply lift her pure white head from it's blanket in the corner of the kitchen.

"And another thing, still living in that modest detached house, with the millions they have in the bank and stashed away in other places, And he's also the majority shareholder in the robot company. He could retire and buy Buckingham Palace and still have a couple of million change. It's a pity you lost your job on the stock market floor, we might have a million in the bank if you hadn't been a greedy fool. And careless! I have thought of an idea how we can make some real money, discuss it tomorrow". Linda ranted aggressively.

"No we won't, I don't want to hear another of your hare-brained schemes, don't involve me. You were as much to blame for me losing my job. You was the one who wanted the grand house in Surrey that we couldn't afford and the top of the range Mercedes, so don't just blame me. And you know as well as me that the robotic factory Is just a front door, and why they've lived

In that house for the past forty years. Your dad is one of the top scientists and mathematicians in Europe but when he leaves that office door, to everybody he's just any other ordinary working bloke. He doesn't go around brandishing his professor or his doctorate titles or the letters after his name. And not forgetting his MBE. No one doubts him working for the robot company, and nobody knows what he really does. And neither do we. Anyway, what's wrong with the house, it's in a fantastic area and has beautiful views of the coast line and the cliffs. It's got to be in the one to two million bracket by now so you couldn't call it modest". Thomas responded showing his irritation and frustration towards his wife.

"Bugger me, look at the time, it's nearly half six, you'll be late for your shift". Linda snapped putting an end to Thomas's conversation.

"One of these mornings I'll go to work in the daylight, what with being on nights again next week, God knows when I'll ever see the sun again". Thomas griped.

"Come on Blanche let's take you to the beach for your morning walk". She called out to the German Shepherd as she approached and slipped the lead onto her collar. Thomas slammed the front door as he followed Linda and the dog out Into the dark depressing morning air.

Linda stopped Thomas in his tracks as he stood by his open car door. "Don't think I don't know what's going on at the hospital". She cried out through the open window of her Mercedes, leaving Thomas rooted to the spot as Linda sped from their concreted front garden 'cum' car park.

Joseph was just reversing his modest car, an ageing inconspicuous Ford Cortina, from his driveway as Linda drew her not so modest Mercedes to a halt alongside her father's vehicle with her headlights illuminating half a mile of coastal road.
"I'm just off to collect your mum from the station, I won't be too long, use your key and let yourself in. Can't stop now". He hollered as he swiftly moved away.

After greeting his wife Jane on the platform immediately she stepped from the train, Joseph promptly relieved her of her holdall and they walked arm in arm out into the gloomy morning drizzle and climbed into the Cortina for the drive home.
Joseph listened intently to his wife's initial grumbling about her tedious journey before interrupting her to ask about their daughter Janine's recent health scare, the reason for Jane's long flight and rail trip back from the south coast.

"Well how was your journey ?" Joseph finally asked and immediately turned the conversation round to discuss the current issue and the revelations on the internet.

"Linda has found pictures on the internet on this Facebook thingamajig of that supposed holiday we had in Switzerland just before I left the army. You remember, when I lost my camera". Joseph quipped.

"Ah well, now she knows, what had she got to say about it ?" Jane replied nonchalantly.

"She thinks you don't know anything about it. She doesn't know anything about your involvement, she doesn't even know you were there, posing as a tourist and staying in the hotel next door. It's been so long ago now I shouldn't imagine it would cause any problem to tell her. She's pestering me to let her contact whoever put it on the internet to try and get the photos and the camera back". Joseph answered with an annoying sigh.

"I agree, I can't see any reason for not telling her the truth about that holiday, we can't be bound by the OSA for the rest of our lives, she's our own daughter for goodness sake". Jane stated.

"I'm afraid we are. I haven't told her, I almost did, I wanted to, and I think she's guessed the rest. She accused me of cheating on you with that Austrian girl,

Elena". Joseph replied causing his wife to chuckle at the thought. "She'll be waiting for us at home, she turned up just as I was leaving, I told her to let herself in. So be warned she'll start on again the minute we walk through the door. You watch". Joseph concluded still never completely losing his black country accent.

Linda wandered to the front garden wall as Joseph steered his tired looking pale grey coloured mark two Cortina onto the drive to be met affectionately by his daughter's very enormous snow white German Shepherd dog.

"Did you have a good holiday Jane ? How is my baby sister now that she's out of hospital and convalescing in luxury in the Hampshire countryside ?" Linda uttered with a hint of envy toward her sister.

"It was far from a holiday Linda, you must realise what she's been through. And the travelling back home wasn't what you could call a picnic. I could only get a flight as far as Newcastle. I had to wait on stand by for that, and then I had a three hour delay waiting for a train. And it's certainly no holiday for Janine after the operation she's been through, and she's desperate to get back home". Jane snapped rebuking her eldest daughter.

"I was allowed to take Janine out for a few days, so I hired a taxi the one day.

We didn't go too far, only a twenty minute ride in the forest to Beaulieu, and another time a couple visiting their daughter were kind enough to take us with them to Southsea and we all took the hovercraft to Ryde on the Isle of Wight for the day. They were lovely days out, the rest of the week I stayed in the hotel grounds with her. The doctor said she'll need a while longer before she'll be well enough to return home. It's costing an absolute fortune in that place, as lovely as it is. She still needs her wheelchair, she'd walk quite a fair distance before she had to use it, so she is getting better. I was hoping to collect her in a couple of weeks, but still, I suppose we have to be guided by the hospital". Jane moaned in dismay. "Anyway, what have you been up to while I've been away?' She added still constantly stroking the white dog without the need to stoop.

"Can I show Jane?" Linda brazenly asked, knowing full well the mischief she was instigating.

"Please stop calling me Jane, what have you got against me? You always called me mum until Janine was born. In my heart you are both equal, both my daughters". Jane pleaded pitifully as she removed her warm dark green overcoat and dropped it over the back of the nearest chair. "Show me......show me what?" She added not waiting or expecting Linda to respond.

"I've already burst your bubble. I told your mum all about the internet pictures on the way home. I knew you wouldn't be able to resist from pestering me to show her. You're like a dog with a bone when you want something, you never let go.....do you ?"

"I've always known about the so called Swiss holiday but I wouldn't mind seeing what my competition was. Your dad did say she was reasonable". Jane remarked while her daughter laid the computer on her lap.

"Reasonable ! Oh my, that's a bit of an understatement Joe, how did you dream that one up ?" Linda replied pretending to cough behind the back of her hand as she instructed her mum to scroll through the pictures.

Having just attained her sixty eighth year and in perfect health, her attractive face at this precise moment looking very tired and beginning to show slight signs of it's years, but enhanced by her head of thick auburn hair contrasting vividly with her stylish pale slim fitting lemon dress as it rested on her shoulders. Jane, although not really in the mood for frivolities, quickly scanned through the complete picture show and closed the computer lid.

"Tart!" Jane pronounced loudly to a spontaneous chorus of hilarious laughter. "She frightened the life out of your dad when we were courting he was a very shy young man, blushed like a beetroot in front of a girl". Jane chirped and reveled in her husband's embarrassment and then realised she had inadvertently acknowledged that she already knew of Elena. "Anyway, no one has offered to make me a cup of tea yet". She added in an attempt at a diversion from her slip of the tongue.

"Hang on a moment". Linda quipped, emphasising every syllable. "I'll make your tea in a minute when you've answered my question......How did you know she scared him. You already knew her, you was there at the same time on that holiday...weren't you? Thomas was right then. He told me he had accidently overheard the two of you reminiscing about having secret meetings during that week and that you weren't supposed to know each other. So you were both on some sort of surveillance, not on holiday at all. I knew it!"

"If that's what you think". Jane said in defiance and gave her daughter a 'mind your own business' look as she handed back the laptop. "I suppose I'll have to make my own bloody tea then". She chirped with a wink and a smile at Linda without any further explanation.

"And what else did Thomas think he overheard ?" Joseph snapped with signs of irritation and anger in the tone of his voice. He stood and lifted his wife's coat from the back of the opposing chair and wandered into the hallway, not expecting Linda to reply.

****

.

Chapter Three

"Hello Jane, is Linda at your place?" Thomas asked with the telephone pressed hard against his right ear.

"No, she's not been round here since I came home last weekend". Jane replied.

"Okay thanks, I'll have a ring round her friends, she can't be far away". Thomas concluded, and after a few telephone calls he restarted his engine to drive the short distance to their home, squeezing his vehicle into the awkward space left alongside Linda's flashy red Mercedes standing askew on the concreted over front garden.

"You've not locked your car". Thomas shouted on entering the house, noting that the driver's mirrors had not been retracted. He closed the front door behind him and again shouted just as loudly, assuming his wife was now back home. "Are you upstairs?" He repeatedly called out her name as he wandered noisily from the kitchen to the lounge, slamming a couple of doors on the way and ending back in the hallway.

"Where the bloody hell are you?" Still no response, Thomas nervously mounted the stairs and stomped in and out of the two bedrooms and returned to the outside on to the drive.

"Morning Mary, You've not seen Linda this morning by any chance?" He asked his neighbour when she appeared in her doorway of their adjoining semi-detached properties..

"No….you've not gone and lost her again ?" Mary joked. "She's probably out walking the dog, was that you making all that din ?" She added.

At that very moment Thomas noticed the dog stretched out along the rear seats of Linda's Mercedes.

"No, she's not out walking with Blanche. The dog's asleep in the back of the car. You know she always takes her in the car to the beach very early, but I don't understand what she's done this morning. It looks as if she's left Blanche asleep and popped to the corner shop for something. That's not like Linda, she treats the dog as if it's her baby. What's she thinking of ?" Thomas snapped and opened the car rear door.

"Come on dog, wake up…..Out you get ! What's the matter with you ?" He screeched as the dog refused to move. "Oh God, I think she's dead". He immediately shouted loudly in a panic to his neighbour the other side of the garden wall.

Mary arrived, scraping her bare arm on the brick entrance pillar in her haste, and began stroking the pure white dog.

"She is alive, I can feel her breathing, I think you need a vet. Perhaps that's where

Linda's gone, to fetch one".

"Why would she have walked, she'd have taken the dog in the car". Thomas retorted slightly disrespectfully to what he considered to be a silly comment. "Will you come with me Mary ?" He then begged apologetically.

Mary inched the dog along the seat and climbed in beside her and began to continuously stroke Blanche's long white hair. Thomas turned the ignition key and started the engine.

"Well the car started, I thought she might have had a problem with it. The key was in the ignition, that's a bit careless for Linda".

Mary made eye contact with Thomas in the driver's internal mirror giving him a severe stare. He then realised that she must have had the same thought regarding the possibility of the car not starting and that her remark was not so silly after all. Humbly he made a more sincere apology.

"Linda told me she had just had it serviced and cleaned when I spoke to her yesterday. In fact we were actually chatting out front when the garage brought the car back, so it should have started". Mary advised Thomas.

"Yes I know it's just been serviced". Thomas replied, slightly annoyed by Mary's knowledge and revealing an unpleasant side of his character. Speedily he reversed the Mercedes from the mass of drab concrete that once used to be the front garden and commented that the vehicle was very low on petrol.

"Well Linda isn't in the vets". Thomas proclaimed in dismay as he returned to the car accompanied by two female receptionists, both very young and slightly built.

"I'll pop back and get some more help". The tallest of the girls offered realising the weight of the dog when they had dragged her along the seat to the open door. After about five minutes of agonising wait while supporting Blanche's head, half hanging out of the car, a stout elderly looking gentleman announced himself as George and that he was one of the vets. With a lot of effort from the five adults, Blanche eventually lay safely on a stainless steel table top.

"My God, this is one heavy dog". The veterinary surgeon gasped, "I know she's been here lots of times but that's the first time we've had to handle her".

"You don't have to tell me, and eat! she takes some looking after, but she's my wife's baby. She couldn't be satisfied with a little Jack Russell or a Scottie, she had to have a German Shepherd, a pure white one. And she couldn't make do with a standard model she had to have the King size". Thomas extorted trying to add a bit of humour to an otherwise unfortunate situation.

"Well let's have a good look at this gentle giant of a dog". The vet announced at the same time ushering all but Thomas from the surgery.

"That blood on her head is from my elbow". Mary quickly informed as she left the room.

After several minutes of examination the vet dramatically suggested that he considered that Blanche had been heavily sedated and decided he would carry out a blood test.

"Has this dog been anywhere this morning ? Or has she been left on her own somewhere ?" He asked abruptly making a suggestion totally unacceptable to Thomas.

"Not as I know, my wife always takes her for a walk on the beach very early every morning, but I've no idea where she's got to. She's always gone out about six, well before I get up. Something must have happened for her to have left her dog in the car like this. She's obviously not phoned here ?" Thomas replied purposefully, not appreciating the vet's tone of voice or his insinuations.

"You get off and find your good lady, I'll know more later, we'll take good care of Blanche. I'll give you a ring when she's awake and recovered enough to go home. She should be well enough by this evening".

"Condescending sod". Thomas snorted when out of the earshot.

"This was on the back seat, Blanche was lying on it". Mary said and handed Thomas a plain white sealed envelope as she climbed into the front passenger seat.

"Oh, what's this all about ? Someone's kidnapped Linda". He screeched holding the note in one hand and the envelope in the other as he slowly digested the one and only short sentence.

"What are you talking about ?" Mary asked leaning across her seat for a look at the sheet of paper. Thomas roughly shrugged away her arm.

"Why...why ? I don't understand, what's going on. Who would want to abduct Linda. What for ?" Ignoring Mary's desire to read the note Thomas quickly screwed it up and thrust it into the door pocket.

"Who's took her ?" Mary desperately enquired.

"I don't bloody well know". Thomas snapped, yet again displaying his aggressive nature, emphasising the word 'I'. "I'm sorry Mary, I didn't mean to shout at you. Please don't say a word to anyone".

"You must go to the police".

"No....no. I can't, and you mustn't say anything. Whoever these people are say I won't get her back if I do". Thomas uttered with a nervous tremor and started the car engine.

"What are you going to do then....are you sure you feel well enough to drive ?" Mary asked seeing how Thomas's hands were shaking as he turned the steering wheel to manoeuvre the Mercedes from the veterinary car park.

"I can't see what the hell I can do until someone contacts me. I'm going to knock on a few doors, see if anyone saw Linda leave the house early this morning".

"I really do think you should call the police. Just in case you change your mind I wouldn't touch this car again once we get back. The police will want to check it over". Mary suggested advocating her wisdom.

"I wonder how come Blanche got to be in the car, and why Linda left her key in the ignition". Mary pondered anxiously.

"Whatever happened must have been when she had just got home or just before she went to go out. She must have already got Blanche strapped in the back of the car and was sitting at the wheel when someone grabbed her. Otherwise the key wouldn't have still been in the car". Thomas stated, still choking with emotion. "Some sod either dragged her out of the car or coaxed her out by asking her something, perhaps directions to somewhere possibly. Why drug the dog ? She wouldn't hurt a fly". Thomas grunted staring back at the vehicle as it stood on the drive.

"There could be signs of a struggle and the police could find some clues. You should call them right away". Mary implored, repeating her request.

"I'll see……,Mary, you go on in, thank you for helping me, but don't you say anything". Thomas reiterated politely.

****

Chapter Four

Thomas arrived in his mediocre silver Volvo at his in-laws cliff top home knowing that he must confide in his wife's abduction and the possibility that her foolishness could be attributed to her disappearance.

His mind was now in a swirl and juggling with a variety of thoughts, while his whole system began showing signs of an imminent breakdown.

Jane greeted him at the door. "What's the matter Thomas, come on in, you look terrible"

"Someone has kidnapped Linda, she's gone missing, someone's taken her" .Thomas blurted out

"What do you mean....who's taken her ....What are you talking about". Jane screamed in disbelief. "She's probably just staying with a friend for the night, you're not exactly the perfect mister and missis these days".

Thomas thrust the kidnapper's crumpled printed note into Jane's hand.

"Oh my God where did you get this ?"

Thomas nervously stammered his way through his ordeal, explaining about Linda's Mercedes being left on the drive and finding Blanche unconscious on the back seat and the trip to the vets.

Jane snatched the telephone handset

from it's base, pressed a key. "Hello". And after several moments of hushed whispering requested. "Will you please page my husband and ask him to come home immediately". Followed by angrily tossing the telephone half way across the room on to the settee.

"Now there must be some reason for someone to want to kidnap her". Jane retorted suspiciously. "What's she been up to ? She always was a little devil, what's she got herself involved in ?"

Thomas reluctantly revealed his own thoughts regarding the internet article. "It might have something to do with the camera that Joseph lost. She wouldn't listen to me...you remember....that Facebook post with those photos. Well she kept on saying that she would like to get it back as a surprise. It's just a suggestion, I can't think of anything else". Thomas replied.

"The stupid girl. That post was a scam to get a response, probably to find our whereabouts. That was ten years ago. Joseph's work was being scrutinised when he was in the army and still has been for the past forty years". Jane paused to consider the wisdom of her next words. "No one ever found the camera. There wasn't a film in the camera, well there was, a new unused roll. Joseph had gone into the toilets to change the used roll of film just before they went on the chairlift, but someone had stolen it. The camera was empty, so they only had the film. So no one has the camera. If anyone did find it, they got themselves a nice camera and a new roll of film". Jane snapped menacingly.

Thomas gave his mother-in-law an ugly stare. "Why on earth didn't Joseph tell us this ? He obviously told you after we'd gone. Oh, I see, you already knew, of course you did, you was there".

"He couldn't say much about it because then it would have led to explaining that holiday". Jane responded making an inverted comma gesture using the fingers on both hands as she uttered the word 'holiday'. "Not that any of this matters now I don't suppose".

"We're not into the official secrets act again, are we ?" Thomas retaliated. "And what was with all the whispering down the phone to get Joseph to come home ?"

"Well unfortunately we are, so for the time being you'll have to accept what we say. Mind you I think we've already gone beyond the boundary". Jane said curtly.

"You've been involved in this all along with Joseph, haven't you ? And all that whispering. Did you have to give a secret code word or a number, it wasn't double o bloody seven by any chance". Thomas snapped being facetious. "You are still working for MI 5". He added in a half hearted joke like manner in order to defuse his anger and the tension of the moment. "And you seem to know all about that holiday".

"No. I am not still in the civil service, but I am still bound by the secrets act, so there's no point swearing at me.....I can't answer your questions. Joseph should be back soon, then we'll contact the police".

"We can't do that, read the note again. I have a feeling that you know who these people are who've kidnapped Linda. It's obviously connected with that film and the holiday in Switzerland. Thomas growled.

"Joseph's here now, he's just driving in". Jane uttered as she stared out of the lounge window. "Let's hear what he has to say".

"I hope this is important, dragging me away from my work half way through the morning". Joseph bawled out the moment Jane opened the door.

"Our Linda has been abducted". Jane answered hastily, and watched as the colour drained from her husband's face.

A lengthy and boisterous argument ensued after Thomas had repeated his traumatic account of the day's events and his conspiracy theories, and the angry confrontation with his father-in-law for not giving Linda his reason to prevent her making contact with the author of the internet article. Desperately emphasising his insistence that the police are not informed.

"Okay, maybe not the police". Joseph chuntered, but insinuating perhaps another organisation.

"This business with the camera was forty years ago, surely it's not still subject to the official secrets act. There wasn't anything but innocent pictures to look at. So why the big secret. You must be allowed to talk about it by now, surely !" Thomas demanded with his voice increasing in volume with each syllable.

"Alright". Joseph relented. "It's been so long ago I don't suppose it's of any consequence now anyway. Linda's the most important thing at the moment". Joseph then proceeded to tell his son-in-law the true reason for that holiday in the Swiss alps including his future wife's role in what turned out to be at futile attempt to expose the hotel proprietors as Soviet spies and to also uncover their contact at the military base.

"Our squabbling and shouting at each other isn't going to get us anywhere or get Linda back. What have they asked you for ?" Joseph urged, pacing back and forth the length of the lounge.

"Nothing yet, here read the letter. It just tells me not to tell anyone or contact the police". Thomas waved the sheet of paper before Joseph snatched it from his hand. "I'll hang on to this letter for the time being, don't destroy anything you receive, and let me see what they're after before I decide what to do". Joseph strictly enforced his demands. "Now bugger off and let me think. Have you tried Linda's number? I don't suppose she still has her phone, but give it a ring. Her whereabouts can be located if she has it, that's if it's still switched on. Bit of a long shot".

"It's ringing". Jane gushed excitedly, intercepting the conversation to make the call.

"It's most likely been dumped". Joseph interrupted.

"Well no one's going to answer it". Jane moaned at her failure.

"Go home and you ring it again. It could be in the house or the car. Let us know either way as soon as you've tried". Joseph insisted.

****

Chapter Five

"Oh damn it". Thomas sighed nervously, seeing what he assumed to be a black unmarked police vehicle parked a few yards from his house. "Damn you Mary, poking her nose". He cried out to himself as his stomach started to churn with fear.

"Mister Langley?" A smartly dressed gentleman asked as he emerged in the dark from the rear of Linda's red Mercedes and calmly introduced himself as detective inspector James Osborne.

A tall imposing person in his mid forties, stockily built with blonde hair neatly parted to the left side. Slightly reddish in the face, probably due to the harsh winter's bitterly cold wind. Attired in a pale grey knee length overcoat and stone coloured trousers.

"Yes.......I am Thomas Langley, can I help you?" Thomas enquired with a look of nervous anxiety.

"We've had a call from 'The Animal Care Surgery' about your German Shepherd dog being doped and the vet mentioned something about you not being able to find your wife. Has she turned up?" James Osborne asked.

For a second Thomas was tempted to say she had returned in an attempt to avoid the police intervention. But decided the truth now would save a lot of very awkward questions later.

"I suggest we go indoors and have a talk". The detective proposed.

"I'm just ringing my wife's number again to see if she left her phone at home". Thomas explained interrupting the detective inspector as he was about to ask a question.

"It could be upstairs or from outside, it's quiet, sounds more like it's coming from the Mercedes". James Osborne suggested. "You stay away from the car, I'll go and see. If there's still any evidence left we don't want it contaminated". After a few moments the detective returned with a mobile telephone held in a tissue. "It was just under the driver's seat, does this belong to your wife ?" He enquired as he unfolded the tissue.

"Yes......that's Linda's. Someone has abducted her, she wouldn't dream of going anywhere without her phone". Thomas responded at the same time holding out his hand to retrieve the item as a trace of tears appeared below his eyes.

"I'm sorry sir, we'll have to keep the phone for a while, we will return it later".

"Have you anyone you need to contact ?"

"Yes, I must ring my wife's parents, I

said I'd let them know if I found Linda's phone".

Thomas then began a full explanation of the whole situation beginning with his wife's obsession regarding the Facebook article and her normal early morning routine and up to the present moment.

Two and a half hours later after extensive questioning the detective inspector James Osborne arose to leave. "As soon as you hear anything from the abductors you must let us know, don't hold anything back or try to go it alone. Forensics will be here first thing in the morning to check the car and the surrounding area. Please don't let anyone go near it. They will be discrete, they may want to remove the car, just depends. I'll say good night to you and let you get on with what's left of it".

"I suppose I'd better give the hospital a call, I'm on night shifts all this week, and I don't feel in the mood and it's a bit too late to turn out tonight". Thomas uttered. "They won't miss me much, I'm only a porter".

****

Chapter Six

With the information regarding the internet post to hand and after being given the transcript of the police interview with Thomas, the Secret Intelligence Service tried but were unable to make contact with the original author of the article.

Following on from this situation a tall handsome gentleman announced himself as Lewis Yardman immediately Joseph opened his front door. Joseph stared at the stylishly attired clean shaven, fresh faced looking young man, waiting impatiently for a little more information.

"Oh...I'm sorry, here". Joseph glanced at his identity card, stared back at the lad's face and let out a disagreeable grunt.

"I was expecting a visit from the police, I assume they must have called on my son-in-law. I suppose you'd better come in agent Lewis Yardman". Joseph replied in a slightly offhanded manner, considering himself superior and at the same time putting the young man on the defensive.

"I'll try not to waste too much of your precious time Mister Showell". He stated with a trace of insolence. "But I've been sent to ask you for all you can tell us regarding your army service, particularly the time you spent serving in Germany. The department are expanding the search for your daughter, they have not managed to contact the author of the Facebook post but a couple of agents have already been briefed and are on location". Lewis added with the intelligence jargon slipping smoothly off his tongue.

"Well if it is to do with this article and they haven't responded they're not going to respond to anyone else either, are they ?" Joseph snapped sarcastically. Then quickly apologised for the sharpness of his comment having respect for the young man's given script and junior status.

"Right then young agent Lewis you'd better sit down". Joseph instructed, now accepting and warming to the young man. "I don't know whether you should be telling me all this, but I'm glad the department is doing something". He murmured as the door bell rang out the chimes of Westminster.

"Thank goodness you're still in.....I forgot my key". Jane moaned as she pushed past her husband and on into the lounge and dropping two heavy shopping bags on to a dining table.

"Oh, you've got company...hello".

"This is agent Lewis Yardman, come to find out what we did in Germany". Lewis quickly stood upright and politely shook Jane by the hand before she disappeared into the kitchen.

"Bring those bags in here for me Joseph". She called back to her husband.

"If you don't mind, we'll wait for my wife, she needs to be a party to this. Make a pot of tea while you're out there". Joseph shouted while in the meantime he took the opportunity to cross examine his inquisitor.

"Where do we start ?" Joseph asked the question to himself. "Yes…I joined the army straight from university in nineteen seventy. I did a couple of months basic training at Aldershot barracks with the two most sadistic lance jacks you'd ever want to meet. Then I spent another few weeks trade training, then informed I was being moved from the REME to the Intelligence Corps. This was when they found out I'd had a university education and graduated with distinctions in all my subjects. I was too embarrassed to let on to my new army mates which university. And after another few months I was transferred to Sandhurst and spent the next two years completing an officer coarse. I passed out in seventy two as Second Lieutenant Joseph Showell, my first step on a rapid rise through the ranks standing to attention with my platoon, in my Sam Browne's waiting for the order to dismiss and scramble off for a well earned pre-posting two week leave.

On our return we all soon learnt our new destinations. Mine was to a science research centre deep in the Black Forest. I was assigned to a team of scientists and designers working on classified projects. That was where I re-met Jane". Joseph murmured as he turned his head to smile at his wife. "She arrived in seventy five working for MI 6 but posing as a typist stroke clerk, in fact you must know all this, you do have records ? She was one of your lot.....Agent Jane". Joseph chirped and again looked across at Jane as she forced a half smile.

"I already knew Jane as a friend from my final year at university, I fancied her then but regrettably I was already married at the time to Iris. So Jane never knew how I felt about her or that I was married. Thank God she came back into my life.

By now I was a captain and was in command of a section, Jane was always hovering and working alongside me but secretly doing her job of monitoring all the personal on the base.

We knew for a long time there was someone on the base who was an informant. We had previously leaked several items of false and immaterial information which found it's way to the Kremlin. So just before I was due to be released to be transferred to a UK ministry position, it was decided that a small group would pose as holiday makers. I was to be in command and we would spend a week at a ski resort near Grindelwald in a hotel known to MI 6 where the proprietors were suspected as being Soviet agents.

Three of us were selected, my best army mate Staff Sergeant Harry Knowles, and Lieutenant John...err...damn, I can't think now what his name was". Joseph stammered as he paused trying to recall the officer's surname. "No, it's gone. I was now Major Showell". He again paused to allow his rapid rise through the ranks to be digested. "Yes, you look surprised, I must admit I was the blue eyed boy. Normally you need at least ten years service to achieve the rank of major. I was promoted only six months before they decided to release me and that was only because of the death of my previous superior. I'm sure with hindsight if they knew that six months later I would be released from the force they would have left me with the rank of captain". Joseph chortled at his good fortune.

"So shortly after Christmas in nineteen seventy eight, three of us travelled by car to Grindelwald and on to the ski resort and to the hotel Gasthaus Rosa. The hotel was run by the Maiers'. Who were , as we were informed, suspected Soviet agents. And as

I said our aim was to try and expose the identity of the person leaking information from the base. My lovely wife Jane, was sent separately in her own capacity and stayed in an adjacent hotel.

Needless to say our arrival wasn't a surprise, they already had knowledge of our mission. So even our carefully pre-planning was known by someone, so the whole operation was a massive flop from the start.

As I was the senior officer in charge of the operation, and although we had no prior warning of their knowledge and so consequently no control over the situation, I took the flak for wasting the whole week, and in not so many words, accused of squandering valuable army finances. On as my Commanding Officer described it. Having a bloody good holiday.

I was due to be shipped back home and released the following week. I was just allowed to cling on to my rank for the sake of my pension, but poor lieutenant Withenhall ....that was his name...it's just came to me, and Knowles'y both got knocked back a rank". Joseph huffed and stopped for a breather.

"I got off lightly with just a severe reprimand from the CO. Blue eyed boy !"
"I'll go and make some fresh tea, you two haven't touched yours, they're cold by now".

Jane said and returned the full cups to the tray.

"Now you say that the Intelligence Services can only assume at the moment that if the author is still around he could be somewhere in the location of our ski resort. Have you received any information back from them since ?" Joseph asked as he picked up his fresh cup of hot tea.

"I'm afraid that's something I couldn't tell you, I wouldn't be privy to that sort information". Lewis replied revealing his junior status.

After a further forty five minutes of personal discussion whilst drinking the tea and consuming a plate of custard cream biscuits between them, Lewis rose from his chair followed by his hosts.

"Thank you for your time and the information, it was a very interesting afternoon. I really enjoyed this last couple of hours listening to your fascinating army careers, you're a great couple. I'm sure we'll find Linda".

"I bloody well hope so, you must keep us up to date, we're desperate for some news of her". Joseph pleaded.

"It's been a pleasure speaking to you Lewis". Joseph uttered as Jane repeated his sentiments.

"I hope you recorded all that information, I wouldn't want to have to do it all again"

Chapter Seven

Thomas not exactly looking his usual suave smooth self, displaying a couple of days of facial stubble quickly drove his Volvo the three miles, returning to his in-laws house. Hastily he climbed from the vehicle and made a dash from the cold into the comparative shelter of the entrance porch away from the biting north easterly wind on this miserable Monday night.

"I had the police round at the house late last night. The vet rang them about the dog being doped and that I mentioned that Linda was missing. I never gave it a thought, obviously he would have to inform the police". Thomas moaned. "So I had no choice, they are involved now and we can't do anything about it. Just hope they don't go blundering around advertising themselves". He said hopefully.

The police wanted your details, so you'll get a visit soon, I'd imagine".

"Yes, I guessed they had, we didn't have the police, we had a young lad from the Secret Intelligence Service pay us a visit with a big red book wanting my life story". Joseph replied with a sarcastic reference to the Eamon Andrews TV program.

"I knew you had someone here earlier, I came about an hour ago, there was a strange car in your drive I assumed it was the cops so I popped back home for a while". Thomas informed.

"You did say you were going to see if any of your neigbours saw anything unusual. How did you get on ?" Joseph asked.

"No joy.....no one said they saw anything, mind you it's still dark around here at nine o'clock let alone sixish when the super woman Linda likes to go jogging with Blanche". Thomas moaned and added. "And I started a week of late nights last Sunday. I finish my shift at four in the morning so I didn't get up until gone ten, so I've no idea if she even went out in her car".

After listening intently to Thomas as he relayed the conversation he had with detective inspector Osborne, Jane, the ever thoughtful host vanished into the kitchen and returned ten minutes later with tea and a bacon sandwich.

"Thomas, sit yourself down and relax for moment. I know you won't have eaten all day". Jane chirped sympathetically and handed him the tea and the bacon sandwich.

Thomas was flustered and began to talk mournfully while chewing his food. "I don't know what to do next....where do you think she could be ? Do you think she's still in the country, still here in Scotland".

"I've no idea, we're not sure if she

did make contact with whoever posted that article. The Intelligence people couldn't get a response, and it was originally put on the internet ten years ago. If she did get through to them it must have something to do with my work for the ministry. The person who stole my roll of film must have something to do with it. It could even be Elena". Joseph gulped despondently.

"Well Thomas". Joseph said letting out a heavy sigh. "There's nothing we can do for the moment except wait until someone contacts you. If it is to do with the internet post, it's probably information from me they're after, so I imagine if Linda is forced to give my details, it'll be me they'll be contacting. What good they think any information I might provide will do them is anybody's guess".

"I'm going to have to see about it, tonight is going to be a long night. I suppose I might as well go to work tomorrow, there's not a lot anyone can do. I'll give the vet a call when I get home. Oh, perhaps not, I might wake him up, it'll have to be tomorrow now. He hasn't rung me so they must intend to keep her in overnight. I could have done with her company tonight". Thomas concluded, and shrugged his shoulders in disbelief that his wife could be the victim of a foreign spy conspiracy.

Jane, elegant and slim, and a year younger than Joseph, stood holding the door open watching Thomas leave.

"Goodness me, it's damn freezing out there tonight". She gushed on re-entering the warmth of the lounge shivering and rubbing her hands.

"If it is what I think, it probably has got something to do with Elena. I assume she is still alive and operating as a Soviet spy or possibly a double agent. They must think they can use Linda to blackmail me into revealing details of my current project. The Intelligence Service are aware of an attempt to access what we're working on". Joseph uttered quietly as if a stranger was in earshot.

"Now the SIS are involved you're going to be closely watched. I know you would never betray your country and give any secrets away, but how are we going to get Linda free when we don't have anything to barter with ?" Jane cried and immediately burst into tears.

****

Chapter Eight

As Thomas had predicted the police presented themselves at Joseph's door the following day in the early hours, well before darkness had turned to light.

"Oh....good morning, I was wondering whether we'd get a visit by the police. We've already had MI 5 at the door". Joseph moaned at the thought of another interrogation as he invited his new guests into his house.

Joseph and Jane began their interview with the detective by giving an in depth history of how they first fostered Linda when she was twelve years old. The details of the conversation being monitored by a plain clothed lady police officer.

"She never knew who her father was, and her mother committed suicide when she was just four. She was then pushed from one unsatisfactory foster family to another foster family and then put in a home until we were allowed to foster her. She was far from the ideal kiddy to adopt but after a couple of years we thought a stable home was what she needed so we applied to adopt her". Jane explained having just told a half truth 'cum' white lie, pausing for a gulp of tea before proceeding.

"I had been told several years before that I wouldn't ever be able to have any children of my own, so I was delighted to be able to call her our daughter. Then three years later we were unexpectedly blessed with Janine. The upsetting outcome is, that up until Janine was born Linda always called us mum and dad. Since then it's been Jane and Joe".

Joseph took over the conversation to explain his roll in the army and the Swiss holiday and leading up to the lost camera and the internet article. "And I think you probably know this and the rest of the events from speaking with our son-in-law yesterday".

"For the time being we can only assume she did contact the author and gave away her address for the delivery, and consequently she was abducted from her own home. Due to the fact that the film was stolen and the purpose of your intended mission in nineteen seventy eight on that holiday in Switzerland, for the time being we can only assume they hope to use Linda to obtain classified information. Unfortunately this means that you and Missis Showell will be under exceptional scrutiny for some time, which I assume you'd expect anyway". The police detective informed in his official capacity.

"Yes......we are well aware of our position and responsibilities. We've already been advised by the Intelligence Service, but there has got to be someway of getting her free". Joseph pleaded.

"I shouldn't really be telling you this, but be warned, don't rely too heavily on the Secret Service Intelligent agents to find your daughter. Their main aim is to dispense with the Soviet agent and identify the informant operating in the UK. Possibly here in Scotland. For some obscure reason they don't consider that Linda has been abducted and if she has, they don't think it's anything to do with espionage".

Joseph gasped at this revelation. "For God's sake they can't just ignore all the facts, everything I told that young Lewis Yardman yesterday. This is insane" . He fumed with rage. "I can't contact these people, will you ask MI 5 to send someone to see me urgently…..not the junior lad, but someone in a high position".

"I will definitely voice my concern, but the SIS is a law unto itself. All I can say is that the police department are still pursuing the line of enquiry that she has been kidnapped and everyone will do everything possible to locate her. Just don't conceal any correspondence or direct contact you might have with the kidnappers. Later today you and your son-in-law will receive a visit from the ministry technical boys to install listening devices to your phones. Remember we will be on the other end so always try to keep any conversation going as long as possible. Is that all okay ?"

"Not really, but I suppose it will have to be, we're in your hands". Joseph replied indignantly in response to the apparent lack of interest by the Intelligence Service.

****

Joseph gasped with exasperation and frustration after enduring a very brief and hostile meeting with a gentleman representing the Secret Intelligence Service. Having been informed, in his opinion, by this overburdening egotistic individual of their suggestion that his daughter had not been abducted, and insinuating that she may be the perpetrator of an ingenious blackmail scheme to extort money from her own parents. Probably with the assistance of an accomplice.

Joseph angrily slammed his front door shut almost before the bearer of this unwelcomed miss-information had cleared the threshold.

Joseph carried on in a frantic rage as he returned to the lounge and to his wife now in floods of tears holding her head in her hands. "This can't be true, what proof have they got to make such a judgement". Jane spluttered through her sniffles and tears. "We all know what she's like when she's got a bee in her bonnet and wants to do something. Of course she contacted the author of that internet article, she couldn't resist it. Thomas said she was determined to get you your camera back, he said she wouldn't shut up about it". She stuttered with her face flushed and streaked with mascara.

"I agree with you but where do we go from here. At least the police still seem to be on our side but they haven't made any progress and she's been missing for three weeks now and we've only had a couple of hoax callers up to yet". Joseph moaned and put his arms around Jane and tightly held her as she started to cry again.

"This is just ridiculous ! She's our daughter, she'd never do anything to hurt us, I know she won't call us mum and dad but that means nothing, it's been going on for years. It's obviously something to do with your work. What if they torture her, is nothing being done to find her ?" Jane screeched and fought to release herself from Joseph's grip and ran upstairs to the bedroom.

Joseph stood vacantly staring out of the French doors on to the rear garden at the leaves and debris that has fallen from a couple of ancient oak trees bordering his property. Now bare and waiting for the spring revival. His brain momentarily shut down and for a few seconds his thoughts drifted away from the present turmoil. This brief relief that he allowed himself turned into anxiety as his mind began to wonder about the possibility of removing the trees to increase their view of the coast and the uproar this would cause, and that the council would never consider it. "What the hell am I thinking about for God's sake". He cursed loudly at himself which brought Jane on to the landing to find out what was going on.

"Nothing love". Joseph called out from the hallway as he grabbed a couple of coats from the hall stand as Jane slowly descended the stairs.

"Put your coat on, we're going out". He ordered his wife manfully. "We're going to pay a visit to the travel agents. We can't afford to do this over the phone or on line. I've had enough, I'm not going to wait any longer, being messed about by a bunch of amateur detectives and James Bond wannabes. I have a damn good idea where to start looking for her. That hotel near Grindelwald, Gasthaus Rosa ! is as good a place as any". Joseph said with his pulse racing with excitement and trepidation and doubt all at the same time.

"You are being stupid now Joe, we can't just dash off like that". Jane stated vehemently. But relising Joseph's seething anger and his determination to pursue his objective as he rammed the Cortina into a disabled bay, being the only space available, and partially encroaching on double yellow road markings, she obediently followed him, almost sprinting into the agent's office.

"We need to get to Grindelwald, what airport do you recommend ?". Joseph asked a smart looking young woman breathlessly.

"I'm sorry, I'm only a customer myself, I don't work here". The woman replied with a smile and returned to browsing through her brochure.

"Fool !" Jane whispered as an equally smart shop attendant called Joseph and Jane over to her desk.

"The nearest airport to Grindelwald I would suggest is Zurich". She informed with Joseph leaning heavily on the corner of the desk, his arms rigid and bearing hard down on the polished walnut surface.

"Zurich", Joseph repeated unnecessarily. "Is it possible I could purchase an open ended return flight to Zurich for tomorrow or as soon as possible please". He enquired, now in a more softer and controlled voice as he regained his normal breathing pattern.

"You'd better make that two tickets". Jane spouted over his shoulder. "No way are you going without me".

"Just the one". Joseph repeated to the young woman seated the other side of the desk.

"You seem to be forgetting my previous occupation. I haven't always been selling icecreams and candyfloss". She butted in assertively. "And please order a hire car to meet us on arrival". She added.

"Well...that's all sorted, we fly the day after tomorrow, now we'll go and call on Thomas on the way home and see if he's available to take us to the station. But I want to pop into Currys first". Joseph chuntered as he swiftly reversed a few feet before speeding away at the sight of an approaching car park attendant.

****

Chapter Nine

"We've been trying to contact Mister Showell, would you have any idea of his whereabouts ?" Detective Inspector James Osborne asked immediately Thomas opened his front door. Thomas's initial thought was to deny all knowledge of his in-laws exodus, but settled on a compromise.

"Yes, as far as I know they've gone down to the south coast to visit their daughter. She's convalescing in a nursing home somewhere in Hampshire".

"Do you know the name of the home or how long they intend to stay ?"

"No, I'm sorry I don't, I think they're hoping to bring Janine home, so it could be anytime. Haven't you tried his mobile ?" Thomas hesitantly asked with gritted teeth, knowing full well that Joseph and Jane will have turned their phones off.

"No one answers, it's not ringing, I wonder why...he must have it switched off". John Osborne replied curiously. "Well if he does get in touch with you, let him know I need to speak to him. He does have my number".

Thomas let out a sigh of relief when the detective decided to leave and quickly closed the door and stared in the hall mirror at the beads of sweat forming across his brow, hoping they weren't apparent a few minutes earlier.

Thomas keyed in a number into his new 'pay as you go' mobile phone that Joseph had provided him the day before when he drove them to the station.

"It's Thomas Joe, where are you ?"

"Hi Thomas, it's Jane, we're driving at the moment. We're about half way, we left Zurich an hour ago. What's the matter ?"

"I've just had that detective inspector Osborne round at the house asking where you are, he wants you to contact him". Thomas shouted loudly as if he was talking to someone on the opposite side of the street.

"There's no need to shout, I can hear you perfectly well. You're not using a megaphone, there's nothing wrong with the reception. Joe just said he can go and whistle, he won't be calling him back. You just say we haven't been in touch if he comes back to you. And you are using your knew phone ?".

"Yes I am…..I told him that I'd driven you to the station and that you were going to visit Janine, and I told him I didn't know anything about the home or when you'd be back".

"Okay Thomas, Joseph will ring you later when we're settled in. I'll say bye for now, I'll probably lose you in a second anyway we're just coming to a tunnel".

"That was a bit of clever thinking by Thomas, to tell the detective that we had gone to see Janine". Jane uttered.

"Clever thinking be buggered. That's what I told him to say. It's the reason I gave my department for having a few days leave". Joseph scoffed and tutted.

"In your position you don't need to give any reason to be absent for goodness sake". Jane scorned.

Two hours after leaving Zurich the couple arrived in the village of Grindelwald, surrounded by the Bernese Alps and in close proximity to the notorious Eiger.

Joseph steered the rented bronze and cream two tone Peugeot 208 away from the village centre and down a quiet lane, stopping outside the Gasthaus Alphorn. A picturesque three storey typical alpine building, white coloured rendered walls to the first floor with ornately carved and crafted and decorated timber beams to the eaves with cantilever timber balconies to first and second floors to all elevations. Eagerly awaiting the arrival of the vibrant red geraniums.

"This looks a nice hotel, it is the skiing season, so let's hope they have a room". Joseph said as he stood with the car door still open exersising his legs. "I did think of going on up the valley and booking into the hotel we used in seventy eight, but then that wouldn't have been the best idea. We'll have plenty of time to have a stroll up to the hotel and go in for a drink after dinner. I wonder if the couple still own the hotel, that's if they're still alive, they'd be in their nineties by now. I can't imagine Elena still being around".

"Never mind worrying about finding Elena at the moment, let's find a room first". Jane quipped.

Joseph and Jane left the dining room and were surprised when the desk clerk called to them as they passed through the entrance lobby on the way back to their room and handed Joseph a sealed buff coloured envelope. The couple stopped and looked startled for a moment.

"It's a bit soon to give us our bill, for goodness sake". Jane griped as she paused half way up the first flight of a marble staircase waiting for her husband to reveal it's contents.

"What's all this about ?" He exclaimed. "Return home, you are not safe here. You won't find Linda here". He read out to Jane.

"So much for sneaking off to the travel agents, somebody knows where we are". Jane uttered. "What do we do now Joe ?".

"She's here alright, they just want us out of the way. Come on wrap up warm, we're going to start looking for Elena".

A small group of boisterous apres-ski drinkers suddenly went quiet and turned to stare, causing Joseph and Jane to feel most uncomfortable and slightly intimidated as they entered the almost deserted hotel restaurant. The noise level gradually resumed after they had satisfied their initial curiosity of the newly arrived strangers.

"Bloody foreigners". Joseph whispered.

"Shhhh..how can you say that ?" Jane snapped slightly embarrassed by his comment.

"What language is that, it's not English". He replied with his Black Country humour and accent still in evidence, and added. "I wonder if the Maiers' are still around".

"Now's your chance to find out, the waitress is coming over to us". Jane said, also in a low voice.

Joseph ordered a bottle of sparkling white wine from the very attractive young lady before he began to engage her in a few minutes discussion of complimenting her on how lovely she looked in her traditional alpine costume.

Jane smartly butted in as she sensed that her husband's line of conversation was more inclined towards flattery and flirting.

"We came here many years ago, in nineteen seventy eight in fact, and stayed at this hotel. We were made very welcome and became very friendly with the owners, a couple named Maier, they would be in their nineties now, they wouldn't still be around by any chance ?". Jane enquired politely.

"I'm sorry, I wouldn't know, That was before I was born". The young waitress replied with a smile but suggested that she would ask Anton to pop in and see us. "He's the deputy manager, he has been here for a long time, he might know".

An elderly gentleman with a slight stooping posture whom Joseph and Jane assumed to be Anton slowly crossed the floor and approached their table just as the young waitress returned with a tray bearing a bottle of wine and a couple of sparkling crystal glasses. She placed the bottle and the glasses on the table and quickly introduced the stooping man and scurried away leaving the couple at Anton's mercy.

"You want to see me ?" Anton asked, rather abruptly, and sounding somewhat annoyed and nervous at being dragged from the security of his office. "You're making enquiries about the previous owners….. the Maiers' I understand…..Why ?" He enquired suspiciously.

"We just hoped we could renew old acquaintances, they were very friendly to us when we stayed in this hotel some forty years ago now. We just wondered if they might still be around". Joseph replied

The old fellow glared at Joseph and Jane making them feel more uncomfortable and anxious than they already were as he bluntly informed them that they were both dead.

"Murdered ! About a month after each other". He said in a hardly audible voice as he glanced suspiciously around the dining room at the few diners and the rowdy party of drinkers on the opposite table.

"Poisoned, both of them !" He whispered and hastily scuttled off back to the sanctuary of his office.

Joseph instructed Jane to stay at the table while he proceeded to follow Anton into his office.

Anton burst into his native tongue telling Joseph that his presence was not permitted and asked him to please leave. Joseph easily resisted Anton's effort to force him back into the corridor.

"I should not be seen or speaking to you, you are both spies,....yes ?"

"No Anton...no we're not, we're just here for a nostalgic weeks holiday and we hoped to reacquaint with some old friends. I had a brief romance with a lovely girl named Elarna and I was hoping to see her again". Joseph uttered sympathetically in an attempt to gain Anton's confidence.

"I was only the booking clerk then. I never had anything to do with Herr Maier's activities, you do know he was a spy ?" Anton asked cautiously.

"No, I didn't know that". Joseph uttered and placed his hand on Anton's shoulder as a comforting gesture, assuring him that he and his wife definitely were purely on a nostalgic holiday returning to a familiar place and that he only knew the proprietors as casual friends.

"They had a daughter, she was the Elarna you mention, but it's Elena not Elarna. Anton informed correcting Joseph's deliberate miss pronunciation that he made in his pretense that they were friendly but not over familiar with the family.

Anton looked relieved when he saw a few of the diners pass his window as they left the restaurant and headed for their rooms. Although Anton now appeared more relaxed, he was still anxious and cautious in his wording.

"Elena". Anton said again. "She had already left and gone to live in Austria with her boyfriend just before her parents died and she never came back. Not even for their funerals". Anton proceeded to explain that he had been employed at the hotel since nineteen eighty eight and that a Russian management group had taken over the hotel in two thousand and six, shortly after the Maier's deaths.

It was obvious to Joseph that Anton was being very careful and deliberate in his manner of speaking now compared with his harsh attitude when he approached their table in the restaurant. Jane's solemn face appeared the other side of the glass screen as she gently tapped on the partly open door causing it to slowly open with Jane nervously peeping through the increasing gap.

Anton put his index finger to his lips as he began to write a note scribbled in a mixture of German and English on a sheet of paper he tore from a pad on his desk, and turned for Joseph to read, repeating the gesture with his finger.

Joseph took the pen from Anton's grasp and added Gasthaus Alphorn beneath Anton's message.

Joseph and Jane returned to the restaurant, now empty except for a solitary figure sat at one of the corner tables still laid up for dinner.

"I would like to go". Jane whispered. "I don't like the way that fellow keeps staring at us".

Joseph quickly finished the remains of his wine and beckoned to Jane with his eyes as he rose from his chair and held out a hand to assist her as he pulled her chair out of the way.

"There is a gentlman waiting in the lounge to see you Mister Showell". The female receptionist at the Gasthaus Alphorn informed as the couple arrived back from their walk and entered the hotel. "Also you have a letter". She added and handed Joseph another buff coloured envelope.

"It's Anton, what's he come down here for ?" Joseph chuntered. "Anton, hello again". He chirped as he and Jane dropped as one on to the opposite settee.

"I'll have to be quick". Anton stated. "I'm frightened, I don't want to be seen here, I really shouldn't have come, I don't feel safe. I think someone is watching my office. Herr Maier was my uncle , and I have a feeling I am suspected of being his replacement. My car is parked just round the corner, I don't want it to be recognised, I need to dash away. Something I didn't tell you. Elena and her friend went to live in Innsbruck, that was what she told me the last time I saw her. I'm sorry I do not know the address and I have never heard from her since. I hope you manage to find her safe and well Mister Showell. Good luck. Don't follow me outside".

"He must have been around in nineteen seventy eight, or Maier told him about me, he knew my real name". Joseph gasped. "I thought there was something familiar about him when he approached our table and I think he recognised me. He scribbled me a note saying Elena's friend was a British soldier from a base in Germany".

Joseph suddenly realised he was still holding the second envelope.

"I seem to keep being given messages on bits of paper". He put his hand across Jane's mouth and indicated a 'shush' with his finger to his lips before opening the envelope and ushered her out of the door and on to the tiled landing.

"It's just repeating the previous note. Saying we must not get involved and urging us to leave immediately. How did they know we were here ?" Joseph moaned at the thought of now being spied on throughout their stay.

Jane took the letter and read silently to herself. "You don't think someone has been in our room ? Who would want to listen to our petty conversations ?"

"Well it's obviously the Intelligence Service. They must have had someone permanently watching our house. Didn't the buggers trust me for God's sake ?" He deliberately said loudly as he re-entered the room.

Before Jane could rejoin her husband in the room he quickly stopped her in the doorway and ushered her backwards and let the door close behind him.

"It could be the fella' from the hotel restaurant who's following us". Jane gasped at the thought, frightening herself.

"Never mind him, you go back in the

room and repack our bags we're leaving right now…...right away. I'll just pop down to the reception and make some sort of excuse and see what they intend to charge us". Joseph instructed assertively.

"Where the heck are we off to at this time of night ?" Jane demanded to know. "Can't it wait till tomorrow ? We've been up since five this morning".

"We're going to find Elena Maier, and hopefully our Linda". Joseph snapped.

****

Chapter Ten

After six hours of continuous driving, except for one ten minute toilet stop, the two very weary travellers arrived at their destination shortly after daybreak.

Jane remained fast asleep sprawled awkwardly across the rear seats, where she'd been for the past two and a half hours since their brief stop. Waking up bewildered and disoriented but just in time to see her husband returning to the car bearing a couple of wrapped breakfast snacks and cartons of fresh coffee. "Oh lovely, I'm famished. Are we here, is this Innsbruck ?"

"Yes. .we've arrived". Joseph replied and climbed back into the driver's seat then reclining it into a more relaxing position.

Jane eagerly gulped away at her coffee, spilling a drop as she opened her mouth to speak. "It's a good job you came back when you did, If I'd woke up and you weren't here I would have been panicking".

"You were okay, the sandwich kiosk is only in the next street, I saw it that's why I parked up here". Joseph chirped.

"Now what do we do next ?" Jane asked as she yawned silently.

"Let's just eat our rolls first". Joseph replied while shuffling in his seat to turn his head to face the rear.

"How do you propose we start to

search for Elena in a town of this size ?" Jane enquired sarcastically.

"Well for a start, we're going to find somewhere to stay". Joseph replied as he dispatched his empty food packet by tossing it over his shoulder into the rear seat floor well, and then promptly started the engine leaving Jane to juggle with the remains of a bacon roll and attempting to sip from her carton of coffee and also fasten her seat belt all at the same time.

Within twenty minutes of cruising the streets the couple booked into the Gastof Beifall, a non-descript building with a modern façade. Joseph thanked the porter with a modest tip before both of them collapsed exhausted onto the bed and moments later were both fast asleep.

By the time the couple woke from their impromptu sleep it was well into the afternoon. After a very late lunch Joseph suggested they check through the local telephone directory. "I assume they do have such a thing".

"She probably goes by a different surname now if she got married, so that's not going to do us a lot of good". Jane remarked. "And it'll be just the same with the registration office. So we're a little bit stumped unless you have any better ideas".

"What else can we do ?, we've got to

start somewhere, there must be some sort of paper trail to lead us to her. Come on let's give it a try, you never know she could still be Fraulein Elena Maier". Joseph replied confidently and set off down the staircase and up to the reception desk to enquire for directions to the town registration office while listening to his wife's moans and sceptical remarks as she clung on to his arm while waiting for the attention of the lady desk attendant.

"That car, the grey one parked on the other side of the square with someone trying to hide behind a newspaper". Jane uttered nervously.

"What about it ?" Joseph asked as he swiveled himself into the driver's seat of their hired Peugeot and snatched at the seat belt.

"I saw it this morning after you came back with the snacks. It was parked on the opposite side of the road from us then. I know it's the same car, the driver's mirror is broken and it's taped up. Do you think someone is watching us ?"

"We'll soon find out". Joseph snapped angrily at the thought of being followed and quickly manoeuvred his vehicle away from the hotel car park and drove in the contra direction, passing within inches of the suspicious car and staring at the stranger behind the steering wheel. After driving a few hundred yards along the busy street he drew to a halt and waited. They only had a short wait of a couple of minutes before the grey vehicle appeared in the Peugeot driver's mirror, slowing down as it went by. Joseph held his wife's hand to stop her trembling, watching intently and nervously as the grey car stopped a further couple of hundred yards beyond. The driver emerged from the vehicle and entered one of the shops and reappeared moments later with a newspaper.

"Yes, I think you are right..... .he is following us. He doesn't seem to be in any hurry to move on. And I wouldn't have thought he needed another newspaper. We'll stay here for a while longer, see if we can sit him out".

"I know I'd only just woken up this morning, but I thought then that he looked a bit like the fella' who was in the hotel restaurant last night, I tried to get a look as he just went past but your head was in the way. Do you think he's the one who left those two envelopes yesterday ? He couldn't have followed us all the way from Grindelwald, surely not". Jane stammered anxiously.

"Well if he did he kept well out of sight or he managed to drive all the way here without any lights. There was only a couple of car headlights behind us the whole journey and that was only when we went through a town. My guess is that Anton told him where we would be heading and the message has been passed on to another agent here in Innsbruck. British intelligence I'd imagine. Or we could be totally wrong and no one's following us at all". Joseph retorted and immediately restarted the Peugeot, and as he slowly got closer, the grey car sped away and was quickly absorbed into the morning traffic and out of sight.

"Lost him, damn! I don't think we're imagining it, we are being watched and now he knows that we know. He's either watching us for our own safety or he wants us to lead him to Elena. I have a horrible feeling about Anton. I think he's a bit more than the hotel deputy manager. I have a feeling he was involved with the Maiers".

"He told you he wasn't involved with the Maier's spy conspiracy, didn't he?" Jane uttered.

"So he said, but he was around at the time and he was their nephew. I can't see the bloke in the restaurant being the same person driving the grey car, but he could be a British agent and passed on the information of our whereabouts, or it could have come directly from Anton....I hope we haven't put him in any danger if he is an agent and working for us.".

The Peugeot crawled to a halt between the only vacant pair of parallel white lines indicating a parking space. Joseph walked with trepidation back to the entrance to the car park and observed that their alleged pursuer in the grey Skoda saloon car was no where in sight before entering the registry office through the large glazed automated door.

The receptionist pointed the couple in the direction of the library room to view the vast amount of ledgers containing the details of the citizens of Innsbruck and the surrounding suburbs.

"Yes Thomas, is something wrong ?" Joseph asked the moment his telephone rang.

"Finally.... I've had a demand, they're asking for two bloody million quid". Thomas blurted loudly. "How do they think they're going to get that sort of money from me ?"

"I thought they would be wanting classified military secrets, not money. I don't understand. It's not you they're interested in, they probably know I can afford to pay. What exactly did they say, was it a man or a woman ?" Joseph asked.

"It wasn't a phone call, I had an envelope on the mat when I came down stairs this morning. I tried to get hold of you earlier but I couldn't get a signal.

The note just demands two million pounds and said details of how to pay to follow. There was nothing written on the envelope so it must be someone close to push it through the letter box by hand in the middle of the night".

"I suppose you'd better let the police see it. Just beginning to wonder a bit now about us being over here. We've had two warnings in plain envelopes telling us to go back home. At the moment we're in Innsbruck and just about to try and find an address for that girl Elena. If it's nothing to do with espionage and someone is using the internet post as a bluff, it could be someone she knows from the stockbroker belt who's kidnapped her for the ransom. She got herself pretty well known when you lived amongst them. Well we're still going to carry on with the assumption that she's here or that someone here knows where she is". Joseph ended the call and finally put Jane out of her misery by reciting as near as possible, word for word, what Thomas had said.

"Well it's all or nothing now, we're here so we might as well keep going" Jane retorted "Let's make a start".

"Search through all the Maiers' first and make a note of any likely looking addresses, assuming she hasn't changed her name". Jane suggested as they sat opposite each other, sharing and separated by a narrow heavily polished oak reference table.

"This is next to useless, I've already listed nine possible E Maiers". Jane griped.

"I agree, I've found six up to yet. Let's stop, no point looking for any more. Let's select half a dozen of the most likely ones and check them out first or we'll be here all night. Make a note of the volume and page number just in case we want to look any more". Joseph muttered with a disillusioned grunt.

"Do you still really think Elena could have something to do with our Linda's abduction ?" Jane asked. Joseph looked unconvincingly into his wife's eyes before offering his reply.

"I don't know anywhere else to look if it's nothing to do with her. I only know it was someone close on that holiday who stole the roll of film".

After four thankless days without any further sightings of the stranger and the grey Skoda with the taped up door mirror, and having fruitlessly checked out the majority of the female Maiers' on their list, and inadvertently including even a couple outside the age range, Jane and Joseph wearily returned to the registry office the following morning to widen their search.

"We agree then….forget the surname

Maier". Joseph instructed as if he was still an army major. "Look for any E Maier hyphenated names……..E Maier - Smith or whatever".

"I don't think you'll find many Smiths". Jane retaliated, lifting and lightening the mood. "Hang on, this means we have to check through the whole alphabet, not just the m's. This is a stupid idea, it'll take a month of Sundays".

"Oh forget it…..put these ledgers back in the cabinet and we'll go back to the hotel and after dinner we'll then do what we should have done in the first place". Joseph uttered to Jane's relief.

"Yes……what I wanted to do at the beginning, look on my Apple Macbook". Jane spouted smugly , beaming with self satisfaction.

****

Chapter Eleven

"Right then, here we go. Try her name in full first, see if anything comes up". Joseph instructed his wife.

"Within seconds the screen revealed two Elena Maiers'. "These are the titled ladies we found this morning, the ones we didn't bother with….there's a couple of Elaine and an Eliza, all with some title or other, but that's it". Jane informed reading the script. "That's all there is from this area, do you want me to start searching the whole damn continent ?"

"The one with the Brussels connection sounds interesting". Joseph chipped in.

"She's an MEP you silly sod". Jane cried. "I'll try what we thought about doing at the registry office".

Joseph watched as Jane typed into the google search bar the words, 'double barrel hyphenated people names with middle name Maier in Austria'. After a delay of several seconds the computer produced just the one match. 'Elena Maier-Knowles and location, Vienna'.

Jane and Joseph stared and gasped simultaneously. "That name…he was your best mate, oh my God, so it must have been him who stole your film".

Joseph was a bit reluctant to accept Jane's assertion. "Not necessarily, I know he had a crush on her, he could have just married her".

"Oh come on ! you don't really think that. Let me see if I can find an address in Vienna". Jane searched for more than an hour before giving in without success. "No. Nothing, just the date when they departed Innsbruck".

"I think this dispels any talk about a bluff. Other than Linda and us, the only other person that knew about the article on the internet must have been Harry Knowles and it was posted in two thousand and eight. Linda must have made contact with him and gave him her address for the delivery".

"Don't say it...do we really need to travel all through the night again. It's well past midnight now". Jane cried.

Observing how tired Jane appeared and considering his over estimated view of his true ability to do yet another six hours driving in total darkness, he walked over to the bed, pulled back the duvet and began to undress.

With their minds preoccupied with their discovery on the internet, sleep was difficult to achieve, and with the thought of an early start, the couple barely managed four hours of peaceful rest before the shrill of the alarm rang out for six am.

To help eliminate the possibility of

having the grey Skoda in pursuit again, Joseph contacted the nearest Hertz car hire to have the highly visible two tone Peugeot replaced with a new less conspicuous vehicle.

Once more they set off on yet another long arduous journey but due to Joseph's lack of enthusiasm and stamina the drive to Vienna took almost eight hours to complete.

"Well we've made it and at least there's not a grey Skoda in sight". Joseph chirped relieved to get from the car and stretch his whole body.

As previously in Innsbruck, the couple booked into the first hotel they came across, flopped onto the bed and within ten minutes were both fast asleep.

"Oh hell, I know you won't believe me but I think that is the bloke from Grindelwald sitting on that bench". Jane uttered with a sick feeling passing through her stomach. "What is he up to. I'm going to confront him and ask him why the hell is he following us". She stated as her temper and her courage began to overtake her nerves.

"Just walk on past and don't let him think that you recognise him. It's probably not the same fella' anyway, you're getting a bit paranoid. If it is him he's a lousy secret agent, worse than James Bond". Joseph joked.

"I don't think it's funny, he frightens me, walk a bit faster".

"I told you, it's not him. Look back, he was just waiting for his wife to come from a shop. Here's a taxi, jump in!" Joseph ordered Jane and he instructed the elderly male driver to take them to an address they had discovered in a regional telephone directory.

"Your new pay as you go is ringing. It must be Thomas, it can't be anyone else". Jane fumbled amongst all the odds and ends in her handbag anxiously trying to retrieve the phone before it went silent. Joseph impatiently snatched the telephone from Jane's hand.

"Yes Thomas.....what's the matter?"

"Ten minutes ago....it sounded like a woman's voice, saying I'm to pay the two million pounds into a Swiss bank account and she'll give me the details in the next couple of days. I asked her to prove that Linda was safe. All she said was that she was for the moment, and refused to say any more. I then asked her why she was demanding money and not military secret intelligence. She just laughed and said she didn't know what I was on about. I asked again if she was safe, but she cut me off".

"This is what makes me wonder about the fella' that we think she contacted, but I suppose he could be asking for money, after all that's what the end game in spying is all about". Joseph retorted.

"Well that's what she told me, so now can I expect another envelope through my letter box in the middle of the night. I can't stand in the window watching all night for the next week, I'm on nights anyway". Thomas responded.

"That woman must know the police will have recorded that call. Linda must have given them her home number. They're not going to be daft enough to call on the house again, they will know the police will be watching it". Joseph said quietly as he noticed the cab driver showing an interest in the conversation.

"Where abouts are you now?" Thomas enquired.

"In Vienna, hopefully on our way to an address we hope will lead to finding Linda". Joseph whispered and closed down the conversation.

Joseph handed the driver his fare plus a few extra euros and stood side by side with Jane outside a three storey modern buff coloured brick built block of flats. Jane pointed to the intercom entrance system. They looked at each other, surprised to see only the one name on the board. But desperately hoping the arduous trip so far would not turn out to be a disappointment.

"How do we do this ? Let's hope it is the right Elena. We can't very well just press the button without some reason to see her after all these years". Jane said wisely as they both jumped backwards a pace as the automatic door began to open.

Joseph stood open mouthed as he instantly recognised the elderly lady whose path he was obstructing.

"Entschuldigen sie mich bitte". The smartly dressed lady requested before bursting into the English language.

"Oh my God, It's Joseph........Joseph Sanderson".

"Anderson". Joseph corrected. "You recognise me then. If it's not too much of an inconvenience can we go inside to have a chat ?" "How could I ever forget you Joe".

"Of course Joseph, but I do not understand your tone of voice, you sound angry. What on earth are you doing here ? how did you find me ? I was just on my way out, but that can wait". Elena replied softly

Although they had briefly met forty years ago, Elena didn't realise who Jane was as Joseph introduced them.

Elena a similar age to Joseph, slightly thicker around the waist than Joseph remembered from when they met in nineteen seventy eight, but still a very good looking woman, even with a few visual facial wrinkles.

"Here we are, sit yourselves down. You do look familiar". Elena quipped casting a inquisitive eye towards Jane seated on a cream fabric sofa in the lavish lounge of Elena's penthouse apartment overlooking the river Danube. Although not at the moment looking blue as led to believe.

"Yes this is my lovely wife, she was my girl friend at the time we met in Switzerland but you have no reason to have known her". Joseph pronounced sharply.

"It really is lovely to see you again but I wish I knew why you sound so annoyed Joe, I'll make some coffee". Elena murmured in order to leave the room for five minutes, hoping that Joseph's attitude towards her will have softened by the time she returns..

"Why didn't you tell her I was in the next hotel to the Gasthaus Rosa ?" Jane asked.

"I just thought the less she knows the better".

"I think we're barking up the wrong tree here". Jane whispered. "She doesn't seem to know anything, I don't think she has anything to do with spying or with our Linda. She seems too nice".

"Don't you believe it, she's a very clever lady. She knows why we're here, she's putting on an act". Joseph responded also in a whisper.

Elena sat down besides Jane while Joseph preferred to stand and pace back and forth menacingly in front of the sofa.

"For goodness sake Joseph, sit down". Jane demanded.

"Where is that scumbag Knowles ?" Joseph suddenly snorted.

"Oh I see why you're angry. You thought he would be here with me. I knew from the first day we met that you wasn't interested in me. But Harry was, so I married him four years later. Don't tell me you've been carrying a grudge against him".

"No course not, I knew he fancied you. I don't care who you married, it's that stupid post on the internet with the photos from the film he stole from my camera before I dropped it. You remember when we were on that chairlift". Joseph snapped.

"That was years ago now, if it was him who took the film. He's gone, been gone twenty years ago. He was putting me in too much danger so I asked him to leave. I couldn't stand living in fear of when someone would find us. We kept moving from place to place". Elena replied and tried to continue her explanation. "How did you find me ?"

"Never mind how we found you....do you know where our daughter is being held ?" Joseph screamed out as his temper got the better of him.

Elena scoured up at him as he rose back to his feet, his face now flushed with rage. "Your daughter? What on earth are you talking about? I think you should go!"

"Calm down Joseph, Elena doesn't have any idea what you're talking about". Jane then slowly and deliberately explained the whole story from seeing the internet post and the disappearance of Linda and how they eventually arrived in Vienna.

"It isn't anything to do with me or that scumbag as you called him. He told me you two were best friends. I'll tell you what you didn't know about him". Elena offered.

"I'm listening, I'm all ears". Joseph snapped sarcastically.

"Harry Knowles was the informer you were looking for when your battalion sent the three of you on that wild goose chase of a holiday to Grindelwald. It was him who was leaking secrets from the base to my father. I'm ashamed to say that my father was spying for the Soviets and also passing the information on to the North Koreans and other secrets to your own people. That's why someone had him killed, Then they killed my poor innocent mother. Now I'm afraid for my own life and my cousin Anton. They may well suspect him now".

"What about Knowles, when did he leave the army, is he still involved ?" Joseph butted in interrupting Elena's flow.

"I never knew anything about his activities at the time. He left the army in nineteen eighty and we got married in eighty two. I didn't find out that he'd been passing on secret intelligence information until we'd been wed for about five years". Elena insisted proclaiming her innocence.

"How did you come to marry him ?" Joseph asked bluntly.

"Well I knew I had no chance with you, you weren't at all interested in me romantically. But Harry was, and I did like him. So we wrote to each other regularly and whenever he could he came over to spend time with me and my parents. Then as soon as he was released from the army he came to stay at my parents hotel and then we moved away to Innsbruck where we were married. A few years later I got to find out about his spying and he wanted to stop, but he knew they would never let him out of their control and he had a dread that one day someone would kill him. It was only because I refused to move anymore that he explained his situation. That's when I got really scared and kicked him out of my flat and my life. To be honest he decided to leave me and he went into hiding somewhere. I've reverted to my own name…Maier".

"Why the hell did he put that post on the internet. You don't know how much trouble that has caused !" Jane asked. "Has he got Linda ?"

"Why do you keep suggesting me or him have anything to do with your missing daughter……..I don't know what you keep going on about and I don't know what this internet post is either. We haven't kidnapped her, why would we ?" Elena snapped back indignantly. "Yes, he was an idiot and if it was him who took the film and posted the photographs it must have been in the late nineties when he did it". Elena paused realising Joseph was about to interrupt.

"It was originally put on there in two thousand and eight, so for some obscure reason it got reproduced a few months ago and our Linda was silly and answered it".

"All I know at the time before I lost track of him was that he was struggling to keep his head above the water, and after being with so many friends during his army career he was then all alone and very isolated. He always said he wanted to get in touch with his old friend Joe. So perhaps it was him who posted it hoping you'd answer him. I know he once put an advert in your local town newspaper to try to find you".

"And where is he now ?" Joseph

quipped.

"I honestly don't know, he could be in hiding anywhere, and the mood you're in I wouldn't feel like telling you anyway". Elena answered determinedly.

"What the hell did he expect to find on the film ? The photos taken on the base were just snaps of me and my mates, nothing more. Stupid idiot. He was even on a couple of them". Joseph cried out in disgust.

"Our daughter Linda saw it and we can only assume that she must have replied to it to get her dad his camera back. Joseph told her not to contact the author because he knew it was a scam. But he hadn't told her that when he lost the camera the film wasn't in it. So he knew no one had found the camera. So it must have been Harry Knowles who removed it".

"He obviously didn't know I'd been in to the toilets to put a new film in the camera or he would never had been stupid enough to put it on the internet in the first place, and we wouldn't be in this mess". Joseph added to complete Jane's assertions.

"I didn't know any of these goings on, I thought I was just enjoying a holiday with three lovely British gentlemen. Anyway it was a bit foolish not to tell your daughter".

Elena snapped, now on the offensive. "You must be going mad with worry, have you heard from the kidnappers ?"

Joseph ignored Elena's question, still doubting her sincerity.

"We were really hoping if we found you that we would find Linda, or you would know something about it. Anton told us you left for Innsbruck. We checked out a few E. Maiers' in Innsbruck, then we gave that up as a waste of time. We came across the name E. Maier hyphenated Knowles moved to Vienna, which set the alarm bells ringing and eventually got us to here. Are you sure Harry Knowles has no part in her disappearance ? We think we were followed by someone from Grindelwald to Innsbruck but hopefully we lost him or he decided we weren't worth his time. We think he was acting as an escort to keep us out of trouble. We had been warned twice on the first night to go back home". Joseph said in a more civilised and less irritable frame of mind..

"I hope so, I hope you haven't led anyone to my door. If he has followed you to Vienna he probably wants you to lead him to Harry. There's no saying what these people are capable of". Elena uttered.

"It looks as though we've come on a fool's errand, where do we go from here ? Back home I suppose. I'm beginning to think the intelligence service were right, we're not going to find Linda here". Joseph muttered embarrassingly. "Oh by the way Elena it's Showell not Anderson, that name was just for the holiday".

"Yes I knew that all the time, Harry told me". Elena replied. "Will you stay and have a meal with me ?" She begged.

"Thank you, but we have booked into our hotel restaurant for dinner. It was good to meet you again after all these years, and although we're rather distraught at being no further on to finding our daughter, I am pleased you have nothing to do with it. Perhaps we will meet again one day under different circumstances. We'll see ourselves out". Joseph concluded, and it turn, he and Jane gave Elena a hug and a kiss on the cheek.

"This is my number, please let me know when you find her, I'm sure you will get her back safe and sound".

In their hotel room relaxing with a glass of wine before their evening dinner, Jane sat on the bed with the computer planning the route to Zurich. "You might not want to do this trip in one day, it looks about a nine hour drive".

"Nearly five hundred miles". Joseph commented peering over his wife's shoulder. "That should be alright" He replied in his usual confident style. "Second thoughts, perhaps not, I'm still feeling the effects from yesterday's journey. See if you can book us into a hotel on line now. It'll save us wandering about looking for somewhere. Find somewhere about two to three hours from Zurich, that will give us an easy ride with plenty of time to catch our flight".

****

Chapter Twelve

"I'll go and put the luggage in the car then we can shoot off straight after breakfast". Joseph announced as he stood with the bedroom door partially open. "Catch hold of the door for me". He requested when the room telephone began to ring. "Answer that Jane".

"It's the car rental company, they say they have a new car waiting for us, the one we were given in Innsbruck should not have left their workshops. Will you pop down and sign whatever it is they need". Jane answered.

"Let's hope it's a Merc. I might as well take these bags now I'm half way out of the door. I'll meet you in the restaurant for breakfast".

"Oh my God. It is a Mercedes". Joseph muttered to himself seeing the sleek black saloon with dark tinted windows stationed in the car park thoroughfare, blocking in his and a couple of guest's vehicles.

Within a matter of seconds Joseph was roughly man handled and bundled into the rear of the Mercedes and speeding away from the hotel, leaving his luggage bags standing upright on the tarmac.

He felt what was obviously a pistol

sticking in his ribs. His mouth dried up with fright and for a few minutes found he was struggling to make any words.

Beside him sat the man with the firearm, a fearsome fellow. A burly bearded man with bushy black hair, and with a facial expression enough to frightened the devil himself. The driver was of a similar build, but clean shaven, Joseph caught a glimpse of his face in the driver's mirror but quickly averted his gaze to avoid eye contact. The woman in the front passenger seat remained facing forward, her head mostly obscured by the extended neck rest. But somehow Joseph saw something vaguely familiar about her. He strained to look beyond her into the right hand door mirror to capture her face.

"It's you….Elena…it was you all along. I knew it ! What's going on, where are you taking me ?" Joseph blurted out in frustration with adrenaline pumping furiously through his veins as he defiantly ignored his guard's attempts to silence him.

"I knew I couldn't trust you, I knew you were a bloody liar, a spy. All that pitiful waffle you spouted yesterday. You tipped off these pair of heavyweight KGB thugs as soon as we left you. So what about Harry Knowles, was he a spy as well, or just a poor besotted admirer you decided to marry ? So he left you !"

"Just shut up Joseph and enjoy the ride, you should never have left the UK. You were a total surprise, you just fell into our lap". Elena snapped smugly without turning her head.

"My wife is back there! Where are you taking me". Joseph repeated, ignoring the pressure of the pistol he could feel almost penetrating his rib cage. "You've not harmed her?"

"No one will touch your wife, it's only you and your intellect we want. From what I saw of Jane she is more than capable of finding her own way home".

Joseph's initial burst of courage had now deserted him as he quietly sat and began to feel his body trembling with fear. He looked to the door handle with the intention of attempting an escape when the Mercedes had to stop, but this idea was immediately thwarted when a pair of slightly soiled handcuffs attached his left wrist to the seat belt.

"What do you expect to get from me?" Joseph demanded as bravely as he could, trying to disguise the croaking of his voice with a couple of short coughs.

Without feeling the need to bend forward and turn to look from between the seats at Joseph face to face Elena chose to reply with an air of formality. "These gentlemen just want to take you for a pleasant drive, so Major Showell, relax and enjoy the beautiful Austrian scenery".

Joseph resigned himself to the inevitable, that he had no chance of escape at the moment. His keepers made no attempt to hide their destination and he soon realised they were heading for the Czech Republic. His thoughts then turned to how he could cause a disturbance and attract someone's attention at the border.

Jane in the meantime had sat at a table in the restaurant folding and unfolding the pristine white linen cloth between her fingers impatiently waiting, but now worrying why Joseph was taking so long to join her. Her initial thought was that he'd decided to pop to the garage nearby and put fuel in the car, but the time had now gone well past all reasonable expectations.

Eventually fearing that he might have been involved in an accident she rose from her chair and ran round to the rear of the hotel, stopping as soon as she reached the steps down to the car park. The sight of their luggage standing behind the car they hired in Innsbruck sent a cold shiver through her spine. Not knowing what to expect she dashed over and looked into the car. Anxiously, with her pulse racing at treble it's normal speed, half expecting to find Joseph collapsed, possibly because of a heart attack or a stroke.

Relieved that he was not in this situation but now even more worried as to what really has happened to him. Panic overtook any constructive thinking and she ran back into the hotel screaming that her husband had been abducted, causing several diners from the adjacent restaurant to appear alongside her in the reception lobby.

"He won't be far away, stop being so hysterical, you're disturbing our guests". An irate male receptionist rudely snapped causing Jane to leap into an uncontrollable outburst of anger and frustration.

"What on earth are you blabbering on about, you bloody stupid little man. Are you the person who rang me to tell me about the exchange of our hired car?" Jane screeched.

The commotion was very near to becoming a scuffle with the receptionist as Jane began to hammer the bell on the counter with her fist, until a very smart looking young woman dressed in a fitted cream suit emerged hurriedly from the restaurant. "Madam what is the matter, why all the noise?" She asked. "I am the hotel owner, can I help you? Why are you crying?" She added sympathetically realising how distressed Jane had become.

It took almost an hour before she managed to convince the hotel management of the situation, and eventually the police arrived a further half an hour later. By this time Joseph and his captors had travelled more than a hundred kilometres away from Vienna.

Jane spent the following two hours explaining their reason for visiting Vienna and their meeting with Elena. The police also questioned the desk clerk regarding the information concerning the change of the hired vehicle.

"There's no reply, we gained entry to the stairs and to her door but no one answered". Reported a police officer who had been detailed to visit Elena's penthouse apartment.

"It must be something to do with her, she's the only person who knew we were here and where we were staying. Joseph told me he didn't trust her, he knew she was a Soviet agent. And she knew who my husband was". Jane cried, interrupting the officer as he was about to continue.

"Officer Enrich has stayed behind in the building in case she returns".

"We'll hand this case over to our intelligence service, they have their contacts and should soon be able to find where he's been taken. In the meantime stay here while we contact the British Embassy to look after you and to get you home, someone should be here to collect you very shortly".

"We do still have a rented car in the hotel car park and our luggage is on the ground beside the car. And we have a flight booked from Zurich tomorrow evening. We were intending to drive there". Jane uttered apologetically and again began wiping away her tears.

"I'll get your luggage brought back into the hotel and don't worry about the rental vehicle, someone will take care of it". The lady hotel owner uttered softly as she placed her arm around Jane's shoulders and guided her to a comfortable fabric armchair in the corner of the lounge. "Now you just sit here and rest and I'll order you some refreshments".

****

Chapter Thirteen

The country side flashed by at seventy miles an hour as Joseph sat without even a glimmer of interest, except for noting the occasional road sign.

The driver suddenly swung the black Mercedes from the roadway and stopped sharply on a grassed verge adjacent to an area of dense forest of exceptionally tall slender vertical trees. Joseph immediately feared for his safety, 'this is it, where am I going ?' he pondered nervously as Elena jumped from the car and ran beyond a few trees and out of sight. He sighed silently with relief. His body guard by his side also decided to exit the car leaving Joseph alone with an open door at his mercy. The thought of making what would have been a reckless dash for the woods was instantly blown from his mind as he gave a tug with his anchored left hand.

Suddenly there was a loud sharp crack that disturbed the forest and the air high above the trees instantly became alive with hundreds of high pitched squawking nesting birds frantically clouding the sky line.

Joseph's companion clumsily stumbled back breathlessly into his seat, slammed his door and the Mercedes roared away with the spinning rear wheels leaving deep ruts in the grass surface.

The fear that now gripped Joseph was at it's limit as he imagined what had just been done. "You've just murdered Elena !" He screamed out loud, only to be winded by a sharp thud of a fist to his stomach, accompanied by a stern instruction to be quiet. Joseph sat silently but fearful for his own fate for the next hour desperately searching his mind for an inventive way to attract someone's attention at the border, not yet knowing that the Mercedes had left the highway and was already crossing into the Czech Republic totally unseen through a lonely shrub lined lane, the lane being no more than a disused overgrown farm track. It was about half an hour later when he saw a route sign that he realised the border was well behind them and that he was being taken to Prague.

The Mercedes cruised through the leafy suburbs and entered through a pair of ornate wrought iron gates and drew to a halt alongside a country style building which Joseph observed to be the Russian Embassy.

Still remaining silent since his beating Joseph was roughly pushed beyond the main entrance doors, whereupon his captors left him standing alone in an imposing austere lobby area.

Eventually, after what seemed like a life time to Joseph, a severely dressed young woman called to him from the floor level above. "Come". She ordered abruptly from her position at the top of the dark oak staircase, then pushing open a matching heavy oak door on the landing, she ushered Joseph into a large office.

"Come Professor Showell, take a seat".

Joseph obeyed his host's request and shuffled nervously into a buttoned red leather wing backed chair. He gazed across the enormous desk with curiosity at the obese individual seated opposite, thinking to himself that this man's stomach suggests that he survives on a very rich diet. With his red rounded face bloated to almost bursting point, Joseph detected something vaguely familiar about him.

"How are you Joe ?" Came his host's calm, friendly and very personal opening address, causing Joseph's mind to slip into overdrive trying to think where and how he knew this person.

"Why am I here, why was I taken from my hotel this morning ?" Joseph asked bluntly, choosing to disregard the familiarity of the large man's question.

"Because we value you intelligence and we want you to stay and work for us Joe". Again, Joseph was puzzled by the personal approach of this person.

"And what if I refuse, I have a wife and daughter at home in Scotland. Will you kill me like you've just killed Elena if I say no ?"

"Oh....Elena, that was unfortunate". He answered without offering any further explanation. "Are you forgetting your other daughter, Linda ?"

"So you do know something, is she safe ?" Joseph responded vigorously. "Do you know me ?, I think there's something familiar about you. Who the bloody hell are you". He questioned aggressively with renewed courage.

"Yes, she is safe.....for now. Don't you recognise me Joe, I have added a little bit of weight, I know". Joseph remained puzzled. "Germany, nineteen seventies, skiing holiday, Grindelwald. Enough clues ?"

"Oh my God no...you're not John, I can't remember your second name. You were with me and Harry Knowles, you were a lieutenant in the Military Police. A redcap. Seems very appropriate for you now".

His host nodded and smiled smugly. "Just John will do".

"So it was you...you was the informer on the base, not Harry". Joseph screeched angrily, standing aggressively from his chair. "No wonder our mission failed. You cunning sod ! And you posed as the informant to try and get the Maiers' to reveal his name".

"What made you think it was Harry Knowles ?"

"Elena told me it was him". Joseph

replied now boiling over with hate for this man. "So you stole that roll of film and put it on the internet".

"That was years ago, in two thousand and eight just after I was given this job as adviser to the Russian Ambassador".

"What were you expecting from your Russian comrades.....some brownie points?" Joseph replied sarcastically indicating his disgust for this traitor. "Firstly release my daughter then we might be able to have a conversation". He angrily demanded.

"Joseph my friend, you are in no position to be demanding any conditions". Redcap John responded emphasising the power he possessed over his old army companion.

"Well Major Joseph, what's it going to be.......you can defect and live in the glorious house that's waiting for you and your family on a beautiful Czech hillside, or be arrested and charged with espionage and spend the next twenty years in prison, or we could increase the charge to murder. Or you could just disappear".

"Sod off...and where will you get your evidence ? and as for murder, how did you dream that one ?" Joseph snapped defiantly.

"Witnesses and documents are easily arranged, and you were allowed a private toilet stop on the way here, I understand". The traitor John replied menacingly, parading his authority over his once senior officer.

"I want you to release our daughter before I say anything. Joseph repeated. "And why are you demanding two million quid ? You've got me".

"I can see we are not going to get anywhere, and what's this about two million pounds". John enquired curiously.

"We don't have your daughter !". John stated emphatically as soon as Joseph had completed his explanation of the situation regarding Linda's reply to the internet post and the financial ransom demand. "We never kidnapped her, why would we ? This has all happened as a big surprise with you presenting yourself like a prize turkey. I posted that on the internet ten years ago, no one has ever replied to it, so someone's using it as a bluff. If we did have her we wouldn't be demanding money, and I know it wouldn't influence you anyway".

Joseph was stunned into silence for several minutes, with his mind in a turmoil, buzzing with the thought that Linda may be involved in her own abduction and be the cause of this whole mess, then just as quickly dismissing the whole dreadful idea.

"Well you seem to have got your reward now...mind you I don't know what information you think I carry these days, I could probably just about remember the basic workings of an industrial compressor. Didn't you know ?, I work for a mechanical handling plant". Joseph chirped with a deal of satisfaction.

"And that internet post is why we're out here and Linda is missing. And no ! Of course I won't defect. There's only one traitor in this room". Joseph cursed, only to raise a scornful laugh from his host.

"It's your choice, but you may be persuaded, so in the meantime I will be lenient then my friend". John said in a condescending but threatening tone of voice. "You will be arrested and charged with spying against the Soviet Union. You will stay here for tonight and tomorrow morning you will be flown to Moscow. After that your destination beyond is up to you. Now how about if I order some refreshments". John concluded smugly.

****

Chapter Fourteen

"Thomas". Jane shouted having spotted her son-in-law across the station car park standing by his Volvo and appearing to be having a heated argument with a stranger.

An elderly railway porter scurried closely behind Jane dragging her pair of wandering wheelie suitcases, one in each hand and arrived at the rear of the vehicle as the boot lid began to rise. Without any fuss the porter loaded the luggage into the car and gratefully accepted Jane's generous tip.

"Have you any news on Joseph ?" Thomas enquired as the bother with the stranger momentarily took a back seat.

Thomas gave Jane a hug as she became overcome with emotion once more and began crying. "It's not good, I don't know where he is, someone kidnapped him from the hotel car park in Vienna. Now I've lost my daughter and my husband. I don't know what to do. Take me home please". Jane pleaded while trying to control her sobbing.

"Who is this young man ?" Jane asked politely as Thomas held open the front passenger door.

"He says he's a freelance reporter and he's checking on a story in this morning's local Express that suggests Linda faked her own abduction".

"What story ?" Jane asked with her mood instantly changing to one of anger.

"I should bugger off if I was you mate, and be careful what you write". Thomas snapped and quickly stood in front of the young reporter as he feared Jane was ready to take a swipe at him.

"The press haven't printed anything about Joseph, have they ?" Jane asked. "The Austrian police told me to avoid telling anyone about it for a few days. What's the point in that when half the hotel knew all about it, goodness knows".

"Now what's this article in the paper you're talking about ?" Jane shouted as Thomas struggled with his seat belt.

"That reporter chap gave me a copy of the Express, it's on the console beside you. I knew absolutely nothing about it until he showed me the paper. Someone has dreamt up this ridiculous story that Linda may not have been kidnapped and that she could have staged the whole thing herself or with an accomplice. Apparently the police are also seriously considering this theory. Just had another hoax ransom demand this morning. This is the second, where do they find my address ?".Thomas called out loudly so as to be heard above the noise of the engine and a large lorry reversing close to his offside. "It's on the second page". He added as Jane started to dissemble the neatly folded newspaper.

Jane quickly read the two six inch deep adjacent columns and also the latest ransom letter and then tossed the newspaper over her shoulder, causing a whimper from the passenger stretched out across the rear seats as the pages spread out around her.

"Oh..sorry Blanche sweetheart, I didn't know you were there". Jane said apologetically to the dog.

"What has started to worry me..... " Thomas began. "A couple of days before she went missing we had a bit of a row over me losing my job. She blamed me for our financial situation. Linda said she had an idea how we could make some money. I told her I wasn't interested in another of her hare-brain schemes. She said she'd discuss it with me later, but she didn't mention it again".

"So are you saying you believe this claptrap ?" Jane snarled angrily directly into Thomas's face. "Things are different now, Elena must have been the one to inform on us, Joseph said all along she was lying to us when we met her. The Russians have Linda somewhere. You haven't told this to anyone....have you ?" Jane demanded.

"Of course I haven't, I never believed a word of it'. Thomas replied curtly.

"Well, make sure you don't". Jane

snapped aggressively venting her frustration out on her son-in-law.

"Are you coming in for a coffee ?" Jane asked as she inserted the key into the front door. Thomas followed and dropped her two bags of luggage on to the hall carpet.

'"No thank you Jane, I'll get on home for a few hours kip, I'm on nights again all this week. You will give me a ring when you know anything ?"

"If the national papers get hold of this, I'll ring that bloody journalists neck, whoever he is....or she !" Jane cursed while standing in her doorway as Thomas reversed his vehicle onto the road. "It's going to be a nightmare when they find out about Joseph as well". She uttered to herself.

****

Although being given extremely luxury accommodation for the night, Joseph could only pace the large bedroom worrying what was happening to Jane in his absence, and with thoughts of Linda weighing heavily on his mind.

The congenial atmosphere that had preceded the previous evening abruptly disappeared with the early morning darkness as Joseph was brutally manhandled into the back of a dark coloured transit van and rushed to the airport.

The rough treatment was repeated a few hours later when he stepped from the aeroplane handcuffed to a burly Russian uniformed soldier, then being unceremoniously dragged into a drab red brick building.

Joseph was led through a maze of never ending corridors and eventually being physically pushed into a foreboding concrete cell, devoid of all the needs for civilised human life. The heavy metal door slammed leaving him shaking with fear at the thought of his fate. He looked in dread at the bare bed with its metal springs, standing against the grey block wall and the solitary folded drab dark blanket, and to his wash area consisting of an enameled metal bowl with one grey towel hanging on a rail. A grubby toilet stood alone in the far corner, all the amenities visible from the spy hatch in the metal door. His luxury items consisting of a small wooden table and chair, all within the confines of four grey concrete walls.

****

It was only a matter of three days before the details of Joseph's arrest by the Kremlin became public knowledge and this, together with the exposure by the local press of Linda's disappearance made the double kidnapping front page headlines in most of the morning national newspapers.

Jane stared with dismay and anger from her lounge window at the number of cameras set up and pointing at her house. With no one to help her Jane suddenly felt a prisoner in her own home when she saw a female police constable pushing her way through the throng and moving the most intrusive cameramen away from Jane's gate.

Jane quickly opened the front door and just as quickly closed it as soon as the police lady had cleared the threshold.

"Hello Jane, I'm Sandra,…….. Sandra Hollins". The police constable announced pleasantly introducing herself. "We'll try and get this lot moved away for you, they are a damn nuisance".

"I'm having a job to sleep without being woken by their noise at six o'clock this morning, I hope they've all got beds to go to". Jane moaned as she entered the kitchen and began filling the kettle. "Tea, Sandra". She shouted.

"Yes please…..Is there anything you need". Sandra asked in reply.

"No I'm fine, I was hoping to go for a walk, but I don't feel like being harassed".

"Do you have a way out from the back ?" Sandra enquired..

"Yes but I'd still have to come round to the front, unless I scramble twenty feet down on to the beach". Jane replied forcing a laugh. "I don't suppose there's any news from Russia, and I don't know what we're meant to do about Linda".

Over a cup of tea the police constable advised Jane that there wasn't any further progress other than she already knew, that the Minister for Foreign affairs was in daily contact with both the Russian and Austrian Ambassadors.

"And what about my daughter?" Jane enquired sheepishly, not wishing to hear the gossip version circulating in the media.

Jane apologised to Sandra for her angry outburst after listening to confirmation that the possibility of Linda being directly involved was at present the main line of their enquiry. "It's not true, I know Linda, she would never do anything like this to us. I know it's not your fault, and I'm sorry again that I lost my temper".

****

Chapter Fifteen

During the next six months the strain began to take it's toll on Jane . Although she welcomed the return to the family home of her birth daughter Janine, Jane grew ever more depressed and on the verge of a breakdown. Already her trim figure was showing physical signs of weight loss.

The media interest was now withering away with just a couple of persistent journalists making a daily appearance outside the clifftop property.

Jane's other concern was for the safety and whereabouts of Linda, especially due to the fact that Thomas has not received any further ransom demand notes since Joseph went missing. Her head tormented with the unthinkable conclusion that Linda could have faked her own abduction or be involved with an accomplice.

"Pass my crutches, come on mum let's go and have our walk". Janine suggested.

As soon as Jane stepped on to the pavement she was obstructed by the only remaining press reporter. Now a familiar figure known as Simon. Having seen him from the very first day, standing with the mass of press men and now a lone figure in all that the weather could throw at him, Jane had developed a sympathetic liking towards him. "Yes Simon…..what are you up to ?" Jane asked abruptly.

Janine chose to recline against the garden wall thinking her mother was about to string the poor lad along with some tale or other, when he almost struck Jane on the nose as he tried to show her the screen on his mobile telephone.

"This has just this second been on the news". He spouted excitedly, knowing he would most certainly be the first person to inform Jane. "It says negotiations with the Russian ministry have been completed for the return of Professor Joseph Showell in exchange for Soviet spy Sergio Almanov. The Russian at present held here in Britain".

Jane snatched the phone from Simon's hand and joined Janine leaning on the wall. Together they began reciting the text and simultaneously burst out crying.

"Is this true ?, Oh my God, I thought the negotiations had collapsed. Oh my God". Jane repeated excitedly..

"That's what's just been on the news. Apparently the KGB seized the opportunity to snatch your husband with the sole purpose to secure the release of their agent". Simon informed as Jane handed back his phone.

"Oh my God".Jane cried, again using the Lord's name as a smile replaced her tears.

"Missis Showell, would you please

give me an interview?' Simon asked very politely. "You know I am a local lad and work for the Evening Echo". He pleaded passionately.

"Yes Simon, I will. You can have the only interview I intend to give. But not until I've officially received the news myself. Then I promise, I will call you. You can print that you spoke to me, but no more at the moment".

With the excitement of his impending first ever scoop the young reporter jumped in to his car and raced away.

Janine handed one of her crutches to her mother and then they linked arms and began to skip in step as they commenced their delayed walk.

****

Joseph was completely oblivious to this new development, never having been told of his impending release. His wall chart hanging on a nail now discarded, his last ' X ' to knock off another day abandoned in despair with his once daily exercise routine. His treatment at the hands of his Russian guards was a mixture of brutality and daily humiliation, together with the constant threats to his life. The lack of any information regarding his family, despite his persistent requests intensified his anguish.

The clatter of the spy hole followed

by the groaning of his cell door swinging open caused Joseph to lift his head from his mattress. "Get dressed". A uniformed soldier snapped sharply.

"What for ? What time is it ?" Joseph asked. Joseph's immediate thoughts flashed back to the callous execution of Elena which haunted him every night, always wondering when it would be his turn.

"Just get dressed". The guard repeated and threw a large serge overcoat in his direction, the coat landing on the stone floor, inviting an aggressive verbal onslaught . The guard quickly became impatient as Joseph grappled with the oversize garment as he was roughly grabbed by the arm and dragged from the cell into the corridor to a waiting second guard, The two soldiers escorted Joseph through the corridors and out of the austere prison building into the chilly darkness of the night and bustled him into the back of a black limousine. The vehicle then travelled for three hours until it reached the Latvian border.

Fearful for his safety and not having any knowledge of the negotiations that the embassies had conducted, Joseph stared out into the darkness wondering if this was his final destination.

Joseph was ordered to remain in the car and became confused observing the sequence of lights that began appearing in the distance

As he continued to stare at the mysterious happenings, another limousine drew along side. The blackness of the night and the dark tinted windows prevented him from seeing the occupants.

"Right, get out of the vehicle". Joseph was ordered and obeyed and instantly he had both his arms held in a vice like grip. At last with his heart pumping wildly with a mixture of trepidation, anticipation, fear and anxiety, he realised that he was about to be involved in a prisoner exchange.

Within minutes he was left standing alone at the border in the glow of a fierce spot light, and for a few moments he stood confused and very scared before being swiftly escorted into Latvia and to freedom.

Joseph stood speechless with his new friends and watched as two more prisoners went individually through the same procedure.

The following evening Joseph's plane landed at Heathrow airport where he was met by a couple of British diplomats. After only being allowed a brief greeting with his wife and daughter and a quick chance to enquire about Linda he was whisked away to GCHQ in Cheltenham to be debriefed, leaving Jane and Janine to return to Scotland by themselves.

Chapter Sixteen

"All I want to do for the next couple of weeks is to lounge about the house and garden and keep away from the press. I've just spent six months of my life holed up in a Russian hell hole. No charge....no trial, and then put to the sword at GCHQ by the Secret Service. They started off being pleasant enough asking me a lot about my treatment and the other prisoners and then it turned to our trip to look for Linda and it all got a bit nasty. Now I've just been informed that my work with the MoD has come to an end. And now to add to my bloody misery Batman and Robin are just coming up the drive". Joseph lamented as he cried out from his position in the bay window watching the two police officers approaching the front door.

"Perhaps now they've pensioned you off we might get to have a holiday at last". Jane chirped leaving James Osborne to listen to muted Westminster chimes from the other side of the door.

"Maybe..... possibly a weekend break somewhere. I've been asked if I would like to take over as company chairman by Glen Robotic Handling Ltd". Joseph muttered with a big grin.

"Oh for goodness sake, you're already the majority shareholder in the company.

Forget it". Jane snapped not appreciating her husband's dry sense of humour.

"Answer the damn door before they wear the chimes out". Jane ordered.

"You know what they're here for". Joseph griped the moment just before he opened the front door, immediately verbally lashing out at the officers.

"We're well aware of the accusations being printed in the papers, and we don't want to hear any more on the subject. So I suggest if that's what you've come here to discuss you might as well bugger off". He blurted out uncharacteristically at the same time baring the officers from entering the house.

"I completely understand your anger Mister Showell, but unfortunately we have to pursue all possibilities and we need to ask you and your wife a few questions to try and clear up any malicious rumours before it all gets out of hand. So do you mind if we step inside out of sight of the cameras ?" Detective Inspector James Osborne politely requested.

"You might as well sit down, I feel this isn't going to be a short conversation". Joseph snapped, still showing his anger at this unwanted intrusion when all he wanted was peace and quiet.

"Firstly I've been instructed to advise you that your trip to find Elena was very unwise and foolish. You must surely realise this to your own cost. Not only did you place your own lives in danger but you potentially put the lives of our agents and others in grave peril as well. You were categorically told by the intelligence services that they were not looking for her on the continent......That said, now for the purpose of my visit".

Half way through the inspector's rant Joseph went into shock mode at the very mention of Elena's name, knowing that outside of the Soviet Union, he was the one and only person that knew of her fate.

Jane and Joseph sat quietly side by side on the settee, by now feeling like naughty school children.

The inspector's interrogation began with a barrage of searching questions. beginning with Linda's wayward childhood days from when she spent several years with foster families and time in a children's home and then finally, fostering and legal adoption by Jane and Joseph.

Her aversion to referring to her new parents as mum and dad as soon as Janine was born, and her resentment towards her younger sister.

Her obsession with football and her deep depressions whenever her team lost.

Her depression at losing the affluent life style of her earlier years of married life with Thomas in their Surrey home, the cause of considerable friction between them ever since moving to Scotland.

"Oh my goodness, that makes the poor lass sound terrible, it makes her seem a right handful. She wasn't all that bad, this was all years ago. She really is a great girl and turned out to be a lovely daughter". Jane said sincerely. "They had a good life and a lovely house in Godalming. I can fully understand them not wanting to leave it". Jane added.

"How did they come to live up here in the Highlands". John Osborne asked.

Joseph would have preferred not to have been confronted with this question and hesitantly replied that his son-in-law had to leave his well paid City job in the finance and banking sector, forcing them to downgrade.

"They had to forfeit their home and lifestyle and we had to help them get back on their feet and they settled on living near to us". He concluded, hoping that answer would suffice...."He wasn't sacked, he was asked to resign. Unfairly we understand, but we don't know the details". Joseph added in response to John Osborne's follow up question.

"It's ridiculous, Linda would never do anything like this to us. She wouldn't have a clue what to do with two million pounds,

where would she keep it ? In her handbag".
Joseph snapped.

James Osborne raised an eyebrow at
Joseph's facetious comment. "Perhaps Linda
wouldn't, but one of her Surrey banker
friends would. It's very strange the demand
notes ceased while you were away".

"If it is, then they have kidnapped her.
And she would never have allowed her dog
to be hurt.......For God's sake !"". Joseph
added emphatically.

Realising the fractious mood his host
was in and so as not to increase the
hostile atmosphere, the detective decided to
forgo any further questioning and depart.

"I think that's all for the time being,
we'll leave you to get on with the rest of
your day. You must need some time to
yourselves after your ordeal". He said calmly
ignoring Joseph's rant.

"Just one question before you go.
Going back six months, when I got back
from Austria a young journalist approached
us with a story in the local daily paper
suggesting that Linda had faked her own
disappearance. This started the whole rumour.
How did he get such information ? " Jane
asked politely.

"Well your daughter has been on the
missing persons list for a long while now
and this information is public knowledge".
John Osborne replied while edging closer to

the door.

"We understand, after being put on a list, of course the press will know, but my wife is asking you about six months ago, who leaked it then". Joseph interrupted.

"Unfortunately I have to admit, it was one of our officers. He was suspended at the time. I can't say any more".

"Bloody hell !" Joseph exclaimed venting his frustration.

"What did you make of all that ?" Jane asked her husband immediately the two officers had left. "It can't be true...can it ?" She spluttered with tears reappearing.

Joseph comforted her with both his arms around her waist and with her head resting on his chest damping his shirt with her tears. "Sit down and I'll make us some tea". Joseph uttered softly.

"I wonder if they've been to question Thomas again. That Osborne chap never said if he had. Thomas has got a worse temper than you, he's likely to fly off the handle and get himself in trouble. You were very rude, but at least you resisted hitting him". Jane chuntered despairingly.

"He'll be in bed now, I'll pop round to see him this evening just before he goes to work". Joseph replied.

Jane and Joseph suffered another of many sleepless nights with the knowledge that the police seemed confident that Linda was involved in her own abduction.

"I don't know how you feel but I couldn't stop thinking all night long about Osborne seeming to agree with the damn newspapers that Linda has faked her own disappearance". Jane cried, easing herself from the bed with water trickling from her tired, reddened sore sleep deprived eyes.

"I'm still not convinced she contacted someone, but why would she do anything like that to us. And she wouldn't ever leave Blanche on her own, let alone harm her. I'm surprised they haven't spoken to Thomas again. If they think our Linda's not on her own, he must be on their list as being a possible accomplice". Joseph replied.

"So it sounds to me as though you're having doubts. You think she is trying to get money from us". Jane snapped harshly in reply to her husband's fading faith in their daughter. Joseph wandered from the bedroom and smartly descended the stairs with Jane snapping at his heels. Dressed only in his shorts and wrapped in a red and black vertically striped house coat resembling an older version of Henry Cooper about to enter the boxing ring. "You don't honestly think she could be capable of doing something like this. I know we've had our problems with her over the years, but no... not this, she just wouldn't".

"I think we should be prepared for the possibility". Joseph chipped in creating an immediate uproar, and after many insults thrown in both directions the couple fell quiet for the next hour, each not wishing to inflame the situation. The tuneful harmony of the Westminster Chimes suddenly broke the silence and responsible for interrupting the sombre mood.

"Not Osplod again". Joseph barked with disrespectful reverence towards the detective inspector, as he sat with his elbows lodged on the pine kitchen table supporting his head.

"Answer the soddin' thing then !" Jane snapped obviously now ready to recommence their row. The first in many years.

"Thomas.....come on in, what's up.....I guess Osborne has been round to see you". Joseph remarked observing the furious expression on his son-in-law's face.

Jane pulled a chair from under the table but noting that Thomas wasn't in the mood for sitting, quietly replaced it.

"The bugger was waiting for me when I got home from work. It seems that I'm under suspicion for being in on a scheme with Linda to extort money from my own family". Thomas blurted out angrily. "Well I've not been accused outright...not yet, not in so many words, but I know what that detective Osborne is thinking".

"He was here yesterday spouting the same theory, I intended to call on you last night but I left it too late. Have you got that last ransom letter with you ? The one you read out when we were driving from Zurich". Joseph asked.

"I've had another one this morning, still the same demand". Thomas replied as he handed it to Joseph to read.

"Have you shown these to Osborne ?"

"He's already got the original of the first note and I gave him this one just now. This is a copy he let me take. He made a snide comment about not receiving any demands while you were away".

Joseph noted the professional wording of the payment details and then passed the type written letter to Jane.

"Our Linda never wrote this, she couldn't even spell some of these words let alone understand what it means". Jane spouted in defiance. "Surely inspector Osborne realises it's nothing to do with you, you're the one they're writing to". She added as conciliation for Thomas.

"Thomas do you honestly think she could be involved ?" Jane asked. "I think he's wavering towards that direction". Jane snarled, pointing and wagging a disapproving finger menacingly a few inches away from her husband's face. "She did contact that damn internet article, she couldn't resist....I know her too well". Jane insisted vehemently.

"Jane….you now know that it wasn't Harry Knowles but that Lieutenant John bloke who first posted that years ago and he said that nobody had replied. Damn Russian puppet". Joseph asserted.

"Who says he didn't sell the photos on to someone else….eh !" Jane retaliated. "Elena told us that Harry Knowles was struggling to keep his head above water".

"Now you're being ridiculous. I thought I'd explained it wasn't Harry who stole the film, it was John. You're getting mixed up again, she was making that up to let us think he was the informant".

"Okay, but where do we go from here. What about her well heeled friends down in the stock broker belt that she used to hob nob with, could she have gone to be with one of them. Did she have any particular friend when you lived there ?" Joseph asked Thomas.

"Why are you still suggesting she's guilty". Jane screamed and grabbed her coat from the hall stand. "I'm off….I can't stand anymore of this disloyalty, I'm taking the car !" She again screamed in a rage.

"No you can't take the car, you're banned". Joseph shouted.

"Just watch me !" Jane grabbed the keys from the window sill beside the front door and fiercely slammed it shut behind her, leaving the menfolk in her wake. She recklessly reversed the Cortina off the driveway and sped away along the coastal road.

"Hell.......what now, I've never seen her like this before, I just hope she doesn't have an accident.........She'll be back when she's had time to calm down. It's a pity you didn't come in the drive and block my car. I've a good idea where she'll drive to, let me get dressed and we'll go and look for her".

"I still believe someone abducted her from our drive early that morning. I agree that she wouldn't even leave Blanche on her own let alone stick a needle in her. That was interesting, what Jane suggested".

"What was that ? Go straight across at the island". Joseph interrupted.

"About the photos being resold. We know that this Russian John was the informer and he sounds like the sort of bloke you wouldn't trust any further than you can toss a caber, so they could be in anybody's hands". Thomas suggested hopeful of a change of heart and an agreeable response from Joseph.

"For God's sake Thomas, don't you start on that theory. No one answered that stupid post. I'd like it to be true myself, it would be better than the alternative. Now follow the coast road again".

A few hundred yards in the distance Joseph could see his car, the only vehicle on this chilly windy day to be on the headland car park. Thomas turned off the road and on to the gravelly area and drew alongside the Cortina.

Jane ignored their approach as she sat glued defiantly to one of the many green wooden benches on the cliff edge, using an umbrella to shield herself from the offshore wind.

Thomas wandered off along the grass road verge leaving Joseph the delicate task of cajoling his wife into a more placid frame of mind. Twenty minutes or so later the couple rose from the bench and walked hand in hand across the uneven car park surface back to the car, leaving Thomas shivering with the cold following in their footsteps. Joseph having offered a proverbial olive branch to restore Jane's trust.

****

Chapter Seventeen

"That's that all sorted then, I've put the suggestion to James Osborne, and he has said it sounds reasonable and he will look into it, so all we can do now is to wait for him to come back to us". Joseph said in hopeful anticipation as he returned the handset to it's base. "If it works, that's if the BBC will allow it, it should take the police suspicion away from Thomas for good".

"I've drafted out what I think the message should say. We don't want to give any personal information away or we'll be inundated with crank calls and hoax junk". Jane chirped and continued to write down her ideas.

Joseph glanced over her shoulder as she bent over the coffee table scribbling furiously. "The first bit reads okay but I think you're getting a bit too long winded. I do like the intro'....'Message for Linda' that sounds positive".

"Detective Inspector, come on in, have you got some news for us ?" Jane gushed as she welcomed her guest into the lounge. "Take a seat". She added, beckoning him to sit in one of a pair of comfortable fabric covered armchairs.

Joseph sat in the other anxiously waiting to hear the inspector's words.

"You must realise this will probably not achieve anything and I'm afraid at the moment our investigations have taken us to strongly believe that Linda, on her own or with or held by an accomplice are the only possible alternatives". James Osborne quietly proclaimed to Joseph's obvious displeasure. This was not what Joseph or Jane had greeted him into their home to hear.

"Okay then….that's your opinion, but what about our suggestion ?" Joseph grunted menacingly.

"It took a bit of influencing by our Chief Inspector, but the BBC have finally relented and will allow their program to be interrupted for a limited amount of time. And it's the department's opinion". Osborne said, emphasizing the last few words.

"How limited ?"Jane snapped.

"A maximum of forty five seconds, and they insist on whichever of you is going to deliver the message must attend the studios on Saturday night at ten sharp, just before the program starts for an audition. Is this something either of you feel capable of doing ? You will be addressing an audience of two and a half million people". James Osborne asked with a distinct hint of a warning.

"I had assumed they would provide

the voice, I thought a newscaster or an announcer would do it". Jane replied, sounding disheartened and nervous at the thought of being the one.

"No, sorry to disappoint you. If you do want a celebrity it would cost you a considerable fee. So if you still want to go ahead with the broadcast, decide which one of you it will be and be at this Glasgow address by nine thirty on Saturday night. That's the name of your contact". And after completing his blunt statement Detective Inspector James Osborne wished them luck as Jane escorted him to the front door.

For the next two hours Jane sat nervously with a hand held recording machine practicing her short speech, with each effort sounding worse than the one before.

"For heaven's sake Jane, just relax, it sounds fine". Joseph quipped assuredly.

"It's all right for you, I'm absolutely petrified just rehearsing, so what the hell am I going to be like on the night? Will you do it?" Jane pleaded, only causing Joseph to smile and shake his head.

"You've heard what my black country accent sounds like when it's played back. I'll be right by your side tomorrow night when you read out your message, that's if they'll let me". Joseph reassured.

"Wait for the red light, okay you're

live on air in twenty seconds Missis Showell". The BBC technician called out.

For those twenty terrifying seconds Jane tussled with her fears and took an enormous deep breath as the light changed, and commenced her infinitely timed speech.

"Message for Linda". She announced with the utmost clarity. "This is from Joe and Jane, we desperately need you back home here with us. Thomas and Blanche are missing you. You are not in any trouble, whatever you need will be here for you. If you're able, please. .please come home. We all love and miss you".

Jane sat motionless and relieved at the studio desk at having received a thumbs up signal from the technician as she listened to the distant echoey voice of Garry Lineker repeat, "Joe and Jane need you Linda" before introducing the program.

Jane removed her head set and wiped the perspiration from her forehead and was then escorted from the small studio to be met by her grateful husband with a kiss on the lips. "Well done....well done, you were fantastic love". He gushed with admiration for his wife's courage to speak so confidently to a live audience.

"Now all we can hope for is that she still watches Match of the Day".

****

Joseph and Jane's dream that Linda would return home dispersed with each day that followed without a single response. Not even a solitary crank hoax to break the silence.

"Well we haven't proved or disproved anything". Jane moaned. "We're still no wiser. I still think it's to do with the internet". Jane added despondently.

"Jane, you must stop harping on about the internet. We've got to face the facts. She was always her own worst enemy when she was down south jet setting. Thomas told us how embarrassing it was when she was always bragging to her rich friends how wealthy her parents are. It's a strong possibility one of those so called friends is her kidnapper, or her accomplice. Anyway Thomas is at the door, let him in".

"I had another demand, this morning". Thomas cried out sounding disappointed, holding it in his hand.

"Two million by midnight next Friday or Linda has watched her last Match of the Day". Thomas blurted out.

"Oh no, what do we do now ?" Jane moaned.

"Don't mention this letter to Osborne, I'll sort something out. All the demands have been mailed in the UK so I think it's time we forget any idea of the internet post having anything to do with it. How do these people expect to be paid. They still haven't given any instructions. Seem like a bunch of amateurs to me ". Joseph said and added. "Let me hang on to the letter for now".

****

During the week following the last ransom note Joseph frequently observed Thomas glancing at his phone or sitting with his laptop open fearing for the worse.

"Hello Joe.....at last ! Read this, it's their payment details". Thomas stammered breathlessly with his chest pounding like a drum as Joseph herded him into his study.
"This note was pushed through the letterbox sometime in the night. It's got definite details on where to deposit the money....It says. Two million not a penny less to be transferred by tonight's dead line. And the word 'dead' is in red capitals. And they say they will ring me tonight at ten o'clock with the account number". Thomas groaned, and stared anxiously and hopefully for his father-in-law's intervention.
"Whoever these people are must have a contact in the area and must know how to avoid being seen. I've impressed this on the police a couple of times but these

notes still get through without them seeing anything. You'd think they'd have someone watching your house". Joseph said and began to read the note silently to himself.

"How do we know that Linda is still safe ?. They've never offered any proof up to yet. When they ring you, tell them, you'll pay the ransom when you have proof that Linda is safe and not harmed. In fact give them my number.....my new mobile number. Tell them if they want the money they must speak to me". Joseph insisted.

"That's cutting it a bit fine for their deadline". Thomas retorted.

"If they want the money they won't worry about the deadline. Anyway what was you saying about the police ?"

"Oh.......just that I've seen the odd copper watching the house during the day, and that's only because they're watching me". Joseph ignored Thomas's comment as he folded the note and put it into his back trouser pocket.

Still grasping at straws, Jane blurted out. "What about that earlier stuff you never mentioned until yesterday, something to do with air defense systems. That all seems to be forgotten now". Jane paused and stared at Joseph but before he could reply she suddenly vanished into the kitchen to attend to a couple of slices of burning toast currently setting off the smoke alarm.

"That was just something put forward to get Joe's attention". Thomas balled out above the din. "They knew I could never pay this sort of cash, but they know Joseph can. Especially as Linda has already told half the county that her parent's are multi millionaires". Thomas proclaimed, watching for any sort of reaction from his father-in-law.

"It would be a help if we really had an idea who was sending the notes. The police haven't come up with any forensic results from the letters or the envelopes . If they have they are not telling us. They're probably still in his bloody intray". Joseph moaned sarcastically.

"How is she taking it ?" Thomas whispered sympathetically with Jane out of earshot and now in the hallway furiously jumping on the spot and flapping with a tea towel at the plastic dome fixed to the ceiling.

"Not very well...not well at all. Linda might be our adopted daughter, but to Jane she's our real flesh and blood just the same as Janine". Joseph informed showing a chink in his own emotions as he was forced to wipe the tears from his eyes.

****

Chapter Eighteen

"Mister Showell........Missis Showell". A police officer in civilian clothing greeted as he and a lady police chaplain were led into the lounge by Joseph.

Both Joseph and Jane looked puzzled to see the police chaplain and began to feel uncomfortable by the unscheduled visit.

"Please don't get up".The young lady chaplain requested, seeing that Jane was about to get to her feet. Tears of fearful anticipation began to trace across Jane's cheeks as the police lady came across the room and carefully sat beside her on the settee. "My name is Lucy ". She added sweetly.

"I'm afraid I have some very bad news to tell you". The police officer murmured reluctantly, before introducing himself as Sergeant Brendon Tapper".

"Oh God, please, no....." Jane gasped having already partly established in her mind the reason for their call.

"I'm very sorry, I wish I didn't have to tell you, but we have found a female body, and I'm sad to say, it is Linda". The sergeant paused for a few moments as the lady chaplain put her arm around Jane's shoulder.

"I don't understand". Joseph butted in. completely bewildered in the knowledge that his daughter had spoken to him on the phone two days earlier and that he had succumbed to their demands and paid the ransom money into a Swiss numbered bank account as instructed. His immediate feelings when he saw the officers approaching the house was one of joy, fully expecting to be informed that his daughter was safe and on her way home. Not that she had been murdered.

"Her body was found three weeks ago". Joseph gasped in disbelief at this statement, still convinced in his mind that this is not Linda, but before he could launch into a verbal attack.

Brendon Tapper quickly resumed. "Yes ......the body was found by a private pleasure boat out fishing at the mouth of the sea loch. Actually only ten miles off shore from this house. The clothing became tangled up in the prop shaft and stopped it's engine. She'd been in the water for many months. We're certain she was murdered the day she went missing".

Jane immediately stood and ran out of the room and out into the garden. Joseph's heart missed several beats as he followed her, shouting loudly for her to stop, fearing she would go beyond the cliff top safety fencing at the bottom of the garden.

Jane dropped to her knees on the

lawn a few feet from the boundary and then fell forward sobbing with her head in her hands and her elbows resting on the ground.

Joseph knelt besides his wife and the chaplain sat down on the grass and together they comforted her and coaxed her back to her feet. After a few minutes of comforting, with Joseph's arms wrapped around her waist Jane slowly walked out of the cool sea breeze and back into the house.

"Is she alright ?" Sergeant Tapper asked sympathetically, having stayed and watched from the patio doors as Jane returned to her seat.

"Can I use your kitchen ?, I'll make her a cup of tea". The lady chaplain stated. Joseph sat close to his wife waiting to hear further information.

"Would it be better if I came back another day Missis Showell ?" The sergeant asked, being concerned for her depressed state.

Jane shook her head. "No, I'm sorry please say what has to be said".

"Yes, she was found three weeks ago but we didn't connect it to Linda at first". Again Brendon Tapper paused to gauge Jane's emotional situation before continuing.

"At the moment we think she was put in the water off a floating pontoon or from a dinghy. There are several small boats laying along the shore line, so whoever did this could easily have rowed out a hundred yards to deep water".

Jane suddenly cried out. "It can't be Linda it can't. These people only wanted the money, they had no need to murder her".

"I would dearly love to agree with you Missis Showell, but it is your daughter. We believe two people were involved, or perhaps one strong person. I'm very, very sorry, I know it's no consolation for you but we will get them". Brendon Tapper assured with a degree of certainty.

"I still don't know how you can be sure it is Linda ? How did this girl die ?" Joseph asked still reluctant to accept the police findings.

"The post mortem indicated that she had received an injection of same sedative that was administered to her poor dog. The German Shepherd survived due to her size. We think she was then placed in the sea. Forensics are not convinced whether the amount injected was enough to actually kill her or if she died from drowning". The sergeant halted at this point not wanting to proceed with any gory details. Unfortunately Joseph insisted on knowing why they were not able to decide.

The room fell silent for a few moments as the lady chaplain placed a tray onto a coffee table and handed Jane a cup of tea.

Brendon Tapper picked up two of the cups and hinted to Joseph to accompany him into the study, carefully closing the door.

"Linda had been in the water for a very long time and the gruesome truth is that there wasn't much left of her. There was some strapping still loosely wrapped around her body so we think she had been weighted down, but whatever they used fell away, probably because of her diminishing size. We did find traces of hardened cement dust in her clothing, so it could have been a bag of cement or a concrete block. Not the cleverest of things to use". The sergeant answered bluntly before apologising again for having to be the bearer of such harrowing information.

"Well how can you be certain it is her ?" Joseph stammered as he repeated his earlier question and returning to the lounge to see how Jane was coping. Sergeant Tapper, having further sensitive information to reveal, reluctantly followed,

Again Joseph broached the subject of identity.

"We ran her DNA through the data base and we found just the one match. I think before I say any more I should have a private word with you Mister Showell".

"No…it's okay, Jane already knows.

She's known since our time in Germany. She desperately wanted children of her own but unfortunately she was told this was impossible so she agreed that we would adopt her". Joseph humbly mumbled out his words as he slumped into an armchair and held his head in his hands to hide his grief.

"In that case Mister Showell, you were the only match, you are the girl's father. It is Linda, I'm very sorry to say". The sergeant announced with an inquisitive stare.

"It's not what you're probably thinking, I must explain". Joseph responded. "I met Linda's mother. Iris, at university. We got married but we were both really too young. The marriage was never going to survive from the start. I joined the army straight from university and the baby was born in nineteen seventy two, shortly after I'd been posted to Germany. Before I managed to get leave to see my daughter I found out from my parents that Iris had took the baby and left the area and gone off with another fella'. I had no one to contact, she told me her parents were dead. Then out of the blue in nineteen seventy six Iris wrote to me and told me this new bloke had done a bunk and left her stranded and destitute in a strange town. But before I could do something to help, the next thing

I heard was that she'd killed herself. So I never saw my daughter for five years. I didn't even know her name. The baby was taken into care and I was only allowed to see and hold her when I went to Iris's funeral. I wanted to have her back there and then, but as I was a single bloke and away in the forces I knew it was impossible, but they did keep in touch with me. When I left the army I applied to have her again. Me and Jane were getting married a couple of weeks later, but they said that Linda needed a stable family environment and that she was already with a suitable foster family. I had told Jane all of this when we re-met in Germany when Jane arrived on the camp just before Christmas in nineteen seventy five. We did already know each other from our days at university".

"So you were in the forces with Joseph ?" Lucy interrupted.

Jane reluctantly forced a smile and nodded her head as Joseph resumed speaking.

"Not really, she was working for MI 6, posing as a clerk typist attached to the MoD and drafted on to our team. Anyway me and Jane got together and shortly after when we were married we managed to persuade the authorities to let us foster her. Linda was twelve then and quite a handful. After a couple of years we were formally allowed to keep her. She had never been told that I was her real father so we kept up the pretense so that in her eyes me and Jane had equal status. Jane always wanted me to tell her". Joseph concluded with a sigh of relief.

"I don't suppose you'll catch anyone for it. How do you know she was put in the sea loch?" Joseph retorted as he rose from his armchair and glaring sternly at the smartly attired sergeant before joining his wife and the chaplain on the settee.

"I'm not at liberty to reveal any of our evidence, it could prejudice an eventual prosecution. I can assure you, we will catch them in the end". Brendon Tapper replied confidently.

"What about Thomas, has he been told?" Jane asked nervously wondering his reaction.

"Our officers are with him now. And due to this new fresh situation Linda's car is being taken to the police compound".

"There can't be much to find now, it's stood on Thomas's drive since she went missing. I thought you'd already searched it anyway". Joseph snapped insinuating at what he considered to be police incompetence.

"It wasn't a murder enquiry then". The sergeant snapped back without offering any further information.

Lucy, who had remained quietly sitting

and holding Jane's hand throughout most of the meeting, looked at Joseph and softly asked if he ever wanted to tell Linda that he was her father.

Joseph sighed heavily at the question and a trace of water trickled down the one side of his face. "I wanted to but I never did tell her. Poor kid, God knows I wish I had". He spluttered, then lifted himself from his chair and managed to reach the kitchen before being engulfed in his own tears.

Sergeant Brendon Tapper and Lucy, the lady chaplain waited silently for a few minutes for Joseph to return to the lounge.

"Again, I wish I hadn't had to come and give you this terrible news. Someone will keep you informed, and I'm very sorry if I have annoyed you at all". Brendon Tapper advised cautiously.

"I'll call round in a couple of days time to see you and have a chat, if that's alright. We can arrange for counselling if that would be something you think you might need the lady chaplain concluded.

****

Chapter Nineteen

Joseph opened his front door to be confronted by Detective Inspector James Osborne, whom he recognised in an instant from his visit a couple of months earlier. He was accompanied by a uniformed male police constable.

"We've already met". James Osborne said and was about to repeat his name.

"Yes …of course Detective Inspector Osborne". Joseph interrupted.

"And this is Constable Hartwell". James Osborne added, introducing his companion.

The two police officers proceeded through the wide hallway following Joseph in to his study. Joseph hastily gathered up a small pile of paperwork from the seat of a green leather wing backed chair and invited the detective inspector to sit, and pulled up an odd dining chair for Constable Hartwell. Joseph promptly sat at his desk on his boson style chair, swivelling through one hundred and eighty degrees to face his guests.

"I assume you have some news?" Joseph asked anxiously, in more of a statement than a question.

"Yes, I've called round to inform you. Oh…where is Missis Showell? She ought to be here to hear this".

"I'm sorry but she's gone into town

with Janine. I dropped them off at the station an hour and a half ago. They won't be back for some time". Joseph answered.

"How is Janine now, I bet you're glad to have her back home". The detective inspector enquired sincerely.

"She's fully recovered now, thank goodness". Joseph replied, getting impatient to hear Osborne's news.

"Well, what I can tell you is that we have arrested two people, a man and a woman for the murder of Linda and for demanding money for her release". James Osborne remarked. "Yes" He replied to Joseph's "arrested ?" exclamation, and then repeated his previous statement.

"Thomas Langley your son-in-law and a Darcey Campbell, a staff nurse working at the same hospital as Langley".

Joseph was stunned into silence for several seconds. "What !!" He screamed and thumped his fist hard on the desk, and winced at the pain he had inflicted upon himself. "Who did you say….my own son-in-law !.........Linda's husband !.........No, I don't believe it. This can't be true, you've made a mistake". Joseph screeched at the top of his voice.

James Osborne remained silent for a couple of minutes to allow his host to calm down and accept his statement.

"Are you absolutely sure about this. It

just doesn't seem real. He was here in this room with me only a week before you found Linda's body. She spoke to us on the phone. He began crying and begged me to pay the ransom. He's been playing us for fools with his acting and false emotions".

"You probably didn't recognise the call from Linda, it was a repeat of a call made some time ago. Langley carefully timed it to play at the appropriate time. This was a callous premeditated murder planned a few months before Linda went missing. The icing on the cake was that internet post. That gave them the perfect moment to act. There was no way they could let Linda remain alive, she would always know her kidnappers and they wouldn't have had a secure place to keep her prisoner anyway".

"I'll kill the bugger with my bare hands, the evil sod". Joseph shouted loudly, seething with anger and frustration.

"What about Linda's dog, is someone looking after her ?" Joseph uttered after he regained his composure.

"The lady next door has taken her in for a couple of days until we find her a home". James Osborne advised

"She's a beautiful friendly dog. She'll be pining for Linda. We'll have her, I'll go over and collect her later, on my way when I go for Jane and Janine". Joseph insisted.

"You omitted to keep us informed with

regard to the ransom call and Linda's voice. I understood we had your telephones and internet calls intercepted. It was a bit foolish of you to use another phone, it could have been very costly". Osborne quipped.

"Nothing could be as costly as losing our daughter". Joseph snapped sharply and twisted on his chair to avoid the detective's stare and to hide his guilt at having been persuaded to hand over two million pounds.

"You probably realise we have had Langley under surveillance for some time. We were wrongly convinced that Linda was his accomplice, and I'm sorry for the hurt this must have caused you. But our intelligence was telling us that with his financial knowledge Langley was the most likely kidnapper, but obviously he couldn't very well abduct his own wife without her involvement. We knew that he knew how to handle a large amount of money and would know where to deposit it away safely, and was quite capable of writing the Swiss banking instructions. We were wrong and again please accept my apologies on behalf of the force". James Osborne said humbly.

"We are certain Campbell injected the sedative into Linda and the dog, although our evidence against her is a bit flimsy at the moment and she's denying everything. And her shift started at two am that morning giving her an alibi. At the moment there's a blame game going on between the two of them. Langley finally had to admit to taking Linda and placing her in the loch but he is still insisting he did not kill her".

Joseph's eyes began to glaze over with water as he imagined his daughters terrible ordeal "And how did he do all this ?"

"We already knew from our previous examination of the Mercedes that it had been serviced and cleaned the day before, and the garage mechanic told us the fuel was down into the reserve. But with the petrol reading still below the reserve we assumed at the time that it had only travelled to the vets, or possibly to the beach as well. Finding Linda's body created a whole new investigation. Langley obviously didn't realise how little fuel he had until he set off for the loch with Linda's body, that's if she was already dead and not just sedated. Is this upsetting you ? Would you prefer me to stop. It's all a bit morbid I'm afraid". Osborne apologised yet again.

Joseph stood from his desk chair and wandered over to stand by the window looking out across his rear garden. He indicated with a brisk wave of his hand for the detective inspector to carry on.

"We think he'd already practiced the route and knew exactly where he was going to on the loch, the low fuel did catch him out and would have been disastrous for him had it not been for a twenty four hour garage about five miles into the trip. He paid in cash and put in exactly ten pounds worth of petrol. Unfortunately neither of the night attendants could remember Langley or the car. We missed the cash petrol receipt first time, but a more thorough search discovered it. It had adhered itself to the inner wall of the driver's door pocket. It was dated for the day Linda disappeared. Anyway when he returned the car to home the fuel gauge was back on to the reserve and so we didn't check the mileage. Initially he insisted he was innocent and none of this had anything to do with him. But forensics found his prints on the filler cap, and he'd already insisted that he had never filled up Linda's car. That's when he finally gave in and confessed. Now of course we have checked and we estimate the Mercedes travelled forty miles that morning, taking into consideration the trip to the vets, give or take a couple of miles".

"Could it have been someone else driving the car?' Joseph blindly asked not really thinking straight.

"He has admitted driving Linda to the Loch, and a stranger wouldn't have returned the car". Osborne quietly uttered, not wanting to embarrass Joseph.

Joseph forced a smile and tapped his forehead as a gesture of foolishness.

"There's not much more to tell. We have recommended that they are both charged with murder and for demanding money with menaces. But that's now up to the COPFS and the lawyers to decide.

"I wish Jane had been here, I don't know how I'm going to tell her". Joseph moaned.

"We will of course let you know when and where the trial is to be held. It will most likely be Stirling". John Osborne advised as the two officers departed.

Joseph closed the door wondering why Constable Hartwell only spoke to say hello and goodbye. 'Suppose he could have been called on as a witness if needed'. He thought.

****

.

Chapter Twenty

"How did it go today ?" Jane asked her daughter as she let herself in through the front door. "Where's your dad ?"

"He's just popped to the garage to fill up for tomorrow". Janine replied. "Well the nurse was acquitted within the first hour".

"No...what happened, surely they know she gave Linda the injection". Jane cried out in disgust.

"Everybody knows she did it, but without the evidence the prosecution had no case and dismissed the charge. She's now being called as a prosecution witness. Turning Queen's evidence, I think they call it. They said she was Langley's girl friend".

"I'll make some tea when your dad gets back, How did the bitch get away with it ?" Jane moaned at the thought of this woman walking free as soon as she's put the boot in.

"To start with she started her ward shift at two am that morning and they estimate that Thomas set off about half past three. The time on a receipt for petrol he bought was timed at three forty four, and her flat mate corroborated her story that she left home at half past one. But it's not to say she wasn't injected the evening before, or her flat mate, who was a bloke by the way, was lying. The police had already questioned her colleges at work and searched her flat. So the case against her collapsed. Thomas Langley kept on shouting at the verdict, and the judge had him removed from court. We had to sit for an hour before they brought him back . And when they put her in the witness box he started again, so the judge halted the trial for the day. That's why we're early".

"You don't look very happy". Jane chirped as her husband handed her a sheath of yellow and white flowers.

"No I soddin' well aint, has Janine told you what happened today ?"

"So his girl friend has got away with it, and now she's going to stitch him up". Jane replied.

"That's about it, the trial should be all over by tomorrow night. I can't see how Langley has any defense at all now. His only hope was that she would be found guilty of the murder and he'd get a lesser sentence. I don't know what the flowers are called, that's all they had at the garage". Joseph answered and flopped back into an armchair.

"They're chrysanthemums.....thankyou'. Jane quipped with a look of surprise at receiving them. "I wasn't expecting you back this early, the dinner will be about an hour". She added.

"Why don't you come with us tomorrow, mum?" Janine asked, only to receive a definite shake of the head from Jane.

As Joseph predicted day three of the trial was almost it's conclusion, with the next day to be taken up with the opposing lawyers addressing the jury. Day one being devoted to swearing in the fifteen jury members and substitutes and preliminaries.

"Well is it all over ?" Jane asked the moment Joseph and Janine entered the house..

"It might as well be, just the lawyers summing up tomorrow. Why they need bother. Nothing is going to make the jury come up with any other verdict than guilty". Joseph said with a hint of anger and satisfaction in his voice.

"So are you going again tomorrow ?" Jane asked her husband.

"No. I can't make that journey again. James Osborne was in court to give evidence today, he'll be there tomorrow as well, so he said he will call me to confirm the verdict".

"Joseph.....Good afternoon it's James Osborne". The voice on the other end of the line announced.

"James thank you for ringing, what's the verdict ?"

"The jury found him guilty of placing her in the loch and demanding money with menaces but they could only find him guilty on a majority verdict for the murder". James Osborne said relaying the court verdict.

"And what does that mean ?" Joseph asked hesitantly.

"A lesser sentence most likely, he'll be sentenced next Friday, he should still get at least twenty years plus another five for demanding money".

Joseph sighed in dissatisfaction at this news. "He's only forty eight now, so if he gets parole he could be out by the time he's sixty five. Why can't they hang the bugger ?".

The detective inspector gave a cough of approval at Joseph's suggestion but refrained from commenting. "I don't think he'll be granted that option".

****

Chapter Twenty One

"Have you read the front page of the Mail this morning ?" Jane enquired, passing the paper across the breakfast table.

"Good, let's hope he bloody suffered". Joseph spouted and handed the paper back to his wife.

"It says that wife killer Thomas Langley died in hospital yesterday morning from a mysterious illness after being admitted ten days ago". Jane read out aloud. "He was alright when you saw him, did he say he felt unwell ? You don't seem very surprised".

"No.. he looked very well to me, still trying to give a show stopping performance as usual when we spoke. I would never have gone to the prison to see the evil sod if he hadn't expressed his desire to show remorse. His councilor thought a meeting would be a good idea for both of us. I wanted to go to kill the sod". Joseph stormed.

"And what did happen, you never spoke about it, and I never asked". Jane replied.

Joseph shied away from his wife's request for information and left the breakfast table. "I'll tell you later, I haven't time to stop now, I'm supposed to be chairing a board meeting at the factory in an hour's time. I'll see you later". Joseph said as leant over and gave Jane an affectionate kiss before leaving by the kitchen door.

"Rotten lousy factory". Jane cried to herself as she looked towards the sink and worktops with the mountain of dirty dishes from breakfast and the previous evening meal. "One day he might agree to buy a soddin' dish washer".

"Joseph, you awake ?" Jane whispered, giving him a nudge in the ribs.

"I wasn't, but I am now". Joseph sleepily replied.

"I can't get to sleep, I keep thinking about Thomas. What happened when you visited him, you still haven't told me".

"I'll tell you in the morning, it's only half four, try and get some sleep. Blanche will be demanding her walk in an hour's time".

"No.....tell me now". Jane insisted.

"Oh for God's sake, I'd only just gone off myself. Oh, alright anything for some peace. I wanted him to face Linda so I took him that large photo of her, the one in the silver frame".

"Did he look at it ?" Jane asked, perched up on one elbow and facing her husband wide awake and attentive..

"You could have come with me, but you refused, he did ask to see both of us, then you would know what happened".

"Tell me !" Jane squawked. Blanche

raised her head from her lying position and peered above the foot of the bed. "Blanche......Back to sleep", Jane ordered unsuccessfully.

"He was annoying me, I knew he was giving his best acting performance as usual. When I handed him the picture he did exactly what I expected him to do, he kissed the glass. He asked me if he could keep the photo, The guard agreed it was okay. I took the photo out and told him the frame had special memories for us, so I was keeping it". Joseph paused for a moment, fully expecting a response from Jane.

"It gave me great pleasure to see his face when I told him his girl friend, Darcey Campbell and her flat mate had vanished and probably so had the money".

"Let's hope it chokes them. And where is the frame now? I know the one you mean, I can't remember seeing it since the day you went to the prison".

"It's on my desk, but the glass is missing, needs a new piece. Don't ask !!". Joseph quipped.

"I wasn't going to". Jane replied.

"I'm wide awake now, I might as well get up. That's enough Blanche, I'll wash my own face....Jane, It's your turn to walk her". "No it's not" "Oh come on then dog, you win. Walkies".

THE END

Thank you for reading my story.
I hope you found it interesting and enjoyable.
I would be very pleased to receive your comments.
You can review this book on Amazon books

Yours sincerely t. a. wood

Current book titles by t.a.wood

"Mary"

"Missis Hooper"

"Two yellow Dresses"

"Message for Linda"

Available on Amazon Books